Sedona's Deadly Secret

Debby Arthur Warner

DISCLAIMER

Sedona's Deadly Secret is a work of fiction, and all characters depicted are created strictly from the imagination of the author. Any similarities are purely coincidental.

ISBN: 978-0-9965828-3-4

Library of Congress Control Number: 2016954188

First edition
Printed in the United States of America

Cover and text design by Laurie Goralka Design

For more information:
gjauthor@gmail.com
www.debbyarthurwarner.com

*In loving memory
of my son, Jody. May your creativity
and sense of humor continue to inspire
others, as you've inspired me.*

Acknowledgments

Being a writer is a process, and telling a story as told to me by my characters, is the easy part. Formulating the story into a format so that my readers can feel and understand what I want to convey is difficult, and I'd like to acknowledge those people who have helped me accomplish just that.

A big thank-you to my support system and dear friends Nona Backlund, Patricia Amadeo, and Terry Pickens, author of *There's a Lot I Forgot About Babies*. I appreciate and value their critiques and input.

I credit my copy editor, Bonnie Beach, for her professional eye and for seeing what I don't.

Thank you Laurie Goralka, for cover and text design, and, Donna Bettencourt, for proofreading.

And to my retired publisher, content editor, and dear friend, Carole London, I am forever grateful.

Chapter One

The morning after her interview with Dan, Kelly decided to hike around Bell Rock in hopes of gaining perspective on what she should do about the job offer. She was intrigued with the opportunity to do something different from what she'd always known as a journalist but, at the same time, she was a little concerned about working for a private investigator—an area where she clearly lacked knowledge.

Climbing up the path, she headed to a large flat rock that was one of her favorite places to meditate and clear her mind. She took off her backpack and laid her head against it; with her knees bent, she surrendered to the tranquility—but it didn't last long. Kelly sensed a presence around her and opened her eyes to see if anyone was near. Raising her head, she looked in all directions. There were a few visitors further down on one of the hiking paths, but no one seemed to be close by. Confident she was alone, she resumed her meditative position. Once again she felt a presence, but this time it was much stronger. She sat straight up to check her surroundings, looking at the ledges above, below, and on either side of her, but no one was there. In the distance, she could vaguely hear the sound of muffled voices from hikers who were probably leaving. The early June's morning sun was beginning to heat up, and Kelly had little time left to relish in her solitude.

Soaking in the warmth she began to once again relax with her eyes closed, head leaning against the backpack. The job offer wasn't the only thing Kelly thought about. She questioned her sudden decision to quit her job at the newspaper and move to Sedona, a place she felt was calling her. She also thought about her friendship with the detective, Joe Conrad, and their chance meeting in Cripple Creek, Colorado, where together they solved the murder of her best friend, Tara. Her thoughts abruptly vanished when she heard giddy laughter coming from a young couple nearby as they climbed up to another level on Bell Rock. Opening her eyes, she saw the young couple and a few other hikers who were on their way down, but she flinched when she saw a man sitting across from her. He was only a few feet away, relaxing on a large rock that rested on the ledge she was on.

"Sorry to startle you," he said. "I was concerned that I was holding up the people behind me, so I decided to stop and rest a while. I hope you don't mind. I'll be on my way shortly."

Facing the sun, Kelly sat up and squinted, using her hand as a shield to keep the sun out. "No need to hurry. I'm leaving. I've been here long enough and it's starting to get too hot for me." She reached for her backpack.

"Before you go, maybe you could answer a question I have about this place," said the stranger.

"I doubt I'd have an answer. I'm fairly new here."

"So am I. Well, actually, I don't live here. I'm visiting my cousin for a few weeks. His wife just had back surgery, and he asked me to come out and help with the kids. I work from home on the computer, so I can do that from his house. I guess I was the most logical choice."

"I doubt I can help, but what was your question?"

"My cousin suggested that when he's home with the kids, I should visit some of the vortexes. I'm from Nebraska, and I have to admit that I know very little about a vortex, other than it's where the earth feels alive and has more energy. But I don't experience or feel a sense of enlightenment as I've been told I might. So I guess my question is, am I missing something?"

In the few weeks Kelly had been in Sedona, she'd hiked almost every day, usually early in the morning or early evening, to avoid the heat. Her two favorite places were Airport Vortex and Bell Rock. She'd heard much about the mystique of the vortexes and how masculine and feminine energies radiated from the earth's surface. Sedona was considered to be a very spiritual place, and people from all over the world came to visit the vortexes. Since each person was an individual, every one would experience different emotions and feelings, she was told. It was also said that the more sensitive a person was, the more heightened their senses would become. Kelly considered a lot of what she heard to be nothing more than myth, but she had to admit that when she was there sitting on a rock and absorbing all the beauty the area had to offer, she felt a serenity like none she'd ever experienced before.

Kelly reflected. "I don't know that you're missing anything. It's all very personal, I suppose. Perhaps what you seek is what you gain. I enjoy hiking the area and meditating on its rock formations. I feel rested and very peaceful when I leave."

"Sort of like 'stop and smell the roses'?" he asked.

"I guess so." She heard other people coming and, as they got closer, the stranger—without saying a word—got up and left. Kelly watched him, thinking that how he was dressed was a little odd. *There doesn't seem to be a rule of thumb or dress code when hiking or exploring vortexes,* she thought. She'd certainly seen all styles of shorts, jeans, and shoes, but she'd never noticed anyone wearing what appeared to be dress shoes. She wouldn't have thought much about the golf shirt and khaki pants he wore, but his polished brown loafers with tassels seemed an odd choice for exploring rock formations. The only item that seemed most appropriate was the red Huskers cap on his head. *He is from Nebraska, and he's only here to help his cousin with the kids, so hiking obviously wasn't foremost on his mind, to each his own,* she concluded.

Once the quietness she reveled in was disrupted, Kelly was ready to leave, but she decided to venture off the beaten path and purposely walk by the old juniper tree. Again, she felt it drawing her near. "What is it about you that seems so mysterious?" she asked out loud, looking up and down its trunk. *In a weird way, I sense you're trying to tell me something, but what?* Walking around the juniper several times, she studied the ground beneath it and shuffled her feet through its small rocks and debris. The sun's rays reflected off a shiny object glimmering from the area where she'd just pushed aside some rocks. She knelt down and with her hands tried to dig the dry solid ground away from it, but the hard surface wouldn't be persuaded. Kelly reached for her water bottle, poured the rest of it around the item, and waited for it to soak in. Looking around, she found a small fallen branch and a sharp-edged rock. She worked the soil with both of them, releasing only part of the shiny object. It was enough so she could see that it was a large knife—the size a butcher would use—but it was what she thought she could see on its blade that caused her to shudder. She needed more water—the ground was unforgiving—and remembered that she had an extra bottle in her backpack. The time she had spent with Joe to solve Tara's murder had created even more curiosity in her naturally inquisitive reporter's mind, but it also instilled a sense of caution. She panned the area around her to make sure no one was watching, then quickly grabbed the water bottle and soaked the dirt around the knife, being careful to avoid getting water on the blade. Once it was free, she took a clean tissue from her pocket and wrapped it around the handle, placing the knife in her backpack. Before leaving, she tried to rearrange the dirt and the rocks as they were when she arrived, hoping no one would notice that the ground had been disturbed.

She had an eerie feeling that she was being watched, and when she turned to leave, she saw the man with the red Huskers cap coming quickly toward her. Something about his demeanor frightened her, and she started to run just as a group of hikers came down the path. He briskly turned in the opposite direction and hurried away, and Kelly followed the hikers until she got closer to the parking lot, then ran to her car. Out of breath and shaken, she could hardly control the keys to unlock the car. Once inside, she locked the doors and sped away, hoping she wasn't being followed. Whether there was any importance to the knife or not, Kelly couldn't be sure, but she felt anxious and had a sense that it had its own story to tell.

Chapter Two

Kelly took several detours on her way home in order to make sure that she wasn't being followed. When she got to her condo, she locked the door and even latched the security lock—something she'd never done before. She didn't scare easily. For the most part, she considered herself to be a level-headed, rational person who could understand most situations. But she was taken aback by the stranger and at finding the knife.

Why was he coming toward me? Did he see me pick up the knife? Was he just curious? There were so many questions going through her head. *Since I just found the knife, did I imagine that he seemed intense? But then why did he leave as soon as the others came?* She stared at the backpack she'd left on the floor by the door. *Do some hikers carry large knives in case they encounter a snake, or even a vicious javalina? That could explain the knife, but not the stranger. I've spent too much time alone since moving to Sedona. I'm becoming paranoid, and that's not like me.*

Taking a deep breath, Kelly went to her computer at a small desk next to the patio doors and googled Bell Rock/mysteries/deaths. She was surprised to learn of three occurrences in the Bell Rock area within the last five years. Two were hikers—both foreigners—and they seemed to have fallen while climbing. The third was a woman in her late twenties, and the caption read: "Sheriff suspects foul play in the death of a local woman from Jerome." The next posting said that the coroner ruled the young woman's death at Bell Rock a homicide. Her attention piqued, Kelly clicked on the article to read the full account. The second paragraph stated that the sheriff's department wasn't releasing information on how the young woman—now known to be Melanie Davies, a native of Jerome, Arizona— died, only that she was murdered. In a statement to the media, Sheriff Matt Gardner said, "We're investigating several persons of interest but until we have a suspect, we will not be giving out any pertinent information that might interfere with the investigation."

The knife! I wonder if it could be the murder weapon? Kelly wanted to take it out of her backpack, but she was concerned about contaminating it even more than it might already have been. She felt she should take it to the police station and give it to the lead detective on the case, but she had a thousand questions going through her mind. *What if they ask me why I was digging around the juniper tree? What if they think I know more than I'm telling them? What if they ask me why I decided to put the knife in my backpack instead of calling the police?* She grabbed her cell to call Joe just as it began to ring.

"Hi, Kelly. You free for lunch? My flight leaves later this afternoon, but I was hoping we could get together before I go. I'd like to see you, and I want to know what you thought of Dan and how your interview went."

"Joe! I was just about to call you. Would you have time to come here to Sedona before you have to be at the airport? I can fix lunch for us. It's important, Joe, or I wouldn't ask. I need to show you something."

Hearing the urgency in her voice, he asked, "What's wrong, Kelly? Are you all right?"

"Just shaken a bit, but I'd rather not discuss it over the phone. I'm probably overreacting, but I'd like to talk with you in person. I need to take care of something, and I'm not sure exactly how to handle it. I'll try not to keep you from missing your plane, but I'd really appreciate it if you could come here instead of me going to Flagstaff."

"Count on it. I'll call the airlines and see if I can change to a later flight, and that way you won't feel rushed. I'll be there as soon as I can."

"Thanks, Joe," she ended the call and resumed her search on the Internet. Seeking more information about the death of the young woman from Jerome, Kelly continued looking for information on the Bell Rock area. After checking one site after another, it became obvious there wasn't much written about the homicide of Melanie Davies. Frustrated, she walked out on the balcony and stared at Bell Rock. While waiting for Joe to arrive, she allowed her thoughts to wander. She reviewed the past several weeks and her decision to leave Colorado and move to Sedona, Arizona. She thought about her editor and friend, Stan, and the *Daily Sentinel.*

Eight weeks earlier—Grand Junction, Colorado

"I still can't believe you're doing this," he said. "You're a reporter, Kelly, and a damn good one, at that! How can you walk away from it all?"

"I wish I had an answer, but I don't. Hopefully I'll figure it out, and then we'll both understand." Her eyes roamed around the office of the man who'd been her editor, friend, and mentor for the past decade. "Stan, I've never doubted for a moment that I wouldn't be as good as I am had it not been for you. I appreciate all you've done for me. Not only did you take a chance in hiring a young novice who had just graduated from college, but you took me under your wing and brought out the best this reporter had to offer."

Her final day at the newspaper was more difficult than she'd anticipated, and she waited until the last moment to say good-bye to Stan. Since the age of twenty-two, the *Sentinel* had been her only place of employment, and now—more than a decade later—she was leaving it all behind.

Standing behind his desk, Stan shook his head, as if there had to be more to Kelly's leaving than what she'd revealed. Kelly walked over and put her head on his shoulder. He put his fatherly arm around her. "I'm going to miss you, kiddo. We all are. I know Tara's death was especially hard on you, and almost losing your own life while solving her murder didn't help. You finally took some much-needed time away from the *Sentinel*—at my insistence—and when you returned, you appeared to thrive on a busy work schedule. But I've noticed a difference in you the past several weeks. The one-year anniversary of Tara's death is approaching ... does that have anything to do with your decision to leave?"

She pulled away and noticed the concerned look on his face. "I wish it was that simple, Stan. Maybe then I might be able to work through what I'm feeling, but I really can't explain my actions." She looked at the door leading out of his office and questioned whether she should tell him what was on her mind. *Why not*, she thought. After all, he knew that side of her all too well. He'd refer to it as a deep-level intuitive trait like none he'd ever seen before.

"Stan, remember after Tara died how I kept having an uneasy feeling that I couldn't explain?"

"Yes, I remember. You wondered if it had something to do with her death."

"Right. Tara's death looked like an accident to the police, but I could never accept that. It was that feeling that drove me. I don't understand why I've been so restless lately, except for the fact that I've been experiencing the same uneasy feeling and it just gets stronger every day. It seems as though I should be somewhere else, or doing something other than what I'm doing, but I don't know what it is. I didn't want to mention any of this because I know it doesn't make sense. The only thing I know for sure is that I have to get away."

"I'd suggest taking a leave of absence, but I realize you've made up your mind. Kelly, you're the best reporter I've ever worked with, and I wish I could talk you into staying. But since I know that isn't what you want to hear, reluctantly I'll say good-bye and wish you all the best. I want you to know that if you ever decide to come back, you'll always have a home here."

She was touched and gave him a hug. "Thank you. That means so much. You'll always be my friend, so don't be surprised to hear from me from time to time."

"I expect to. I'd be disappointed if you didn't keep in touch. Kelly, this goes without saying, but if I can be of help in any way—information, reference, whatever—don't hesitate to let me know."

"Stan, you've always made me feel like family, and that's what makes this all the more difficult." She kissed him on the cheek, turned, and walked toward the door.

"You *are* family," he said. "Don't ever forget that." Kelly's hand was on the doorknob when he asked his last question. "Are you still in touch with Joe Conrad? If you are, does he know you're leaving the *Sentinel?*"

She turned. "I haven't talked to Joe for several weeks. He was working on a high-profile kidnapping case and was even out of the country for a while. He has no idea what I'm doing. If he did, he'd probably think I was out of my mind. Who knows, Stan, maybe I am. Only time will tell."

Chapter Three

Six weeks earlier—Sedona, Arizona

Years ago, when Kelly first visited Sedona, she instantly fell in love with the red rock formations and vowed one day to return, but she never expected to be there for an extended period of time.

The condo she found to rent was a comfortable two-bedroom unit on the second floor. Kelly felt fortunate that she could see Bell Rock from the sliding doors in her living room as well as from her back deck. The complex didn't have an elevator, but she didn't mind the steps, and the views were worth the climb.

After finishing her hike on Bell Rock—it was the third morning in a row that she was drawn to hike there—she felt compelled to stop and rest by one of the juniper trees she'd noticed on the other side of some low wire fencing along the path. She remembered reading that juniper trees revealed where the energy is the strongest. Studying the tree, she observed how twisted it was, and she found it to be quite stunning. She'd also read about the Bell Rock Vortex that it strengthened both the masculine and feminine sides and gave balance. She admired the twisted juniper longer than she'd realized, and the temperature had risen. She knew she needed to get back, but she hated to leave. As she walked away, she had a strange sensation that the tree was trying to tell her something, almost as if its twisted branches had a secret to tell. Dismissing the thought, she shook her head and started home.

Her cell phone was ringing when she opened the door. Surprised to see that it was Joe, she didn't hesitate to answer. "Hi, Joe. Are you back in town?"

"Yeah, I got in late last night."

"How did everything go? Were you able to find the child?"

"Yes, in London, but only after his father paid a huge ransom. Thankfully, he was unharmed. Scotland Yard will take over completely now. The kidnapper—or kidnappers, as the boy has indicated—are still on the loose. My involvement is over now, but not before it took me through Scotland, France, and finally London. It's the biggest case I've ever worked on, and I hope I never see one like it again. The only reason I got involved in the first place was because his father and I go back a long way, even before I joined the police force. He knew I'd left the department and became a private investigator, and when he asked for my help, I couldn't say no. I wasn't sure we'd find the kid alive, and I doubt that the family will ever feel safe. He's even hired bodyguards for added protection."

"I can understand his concerns. It makes you wonder if being that rich is worth it. I'm just glad it ended well and that you arrived home safely."

"Kelly, I tried to reach you at the *Sentinel* before calling your cell. When I was told you didn't work there anymore, I asked to speak to Stan. He was pretty evasive and suggested I call you and let *you* explain why you left the paper. It was certainly the last thing I expected to hear."

"I'm sure it was."

"The only reason I can think of for your leaving a job you obviously loved is that you must be seriously ill. Are you, Kelly?"

Oh, geez, he thinks I have a terminal illness. I almost wish I did! At least it would be easier to explain. "No, Joe, I'm not ill—just restless. I've been that way for some time now and I felt the need to move in a different direction—although, as of yet, I'm not sure what direction that is. I just knew I needed some distance between me and the *Sentinel* to figure it out."

"That's a pretty drastic move, don't you think?"

"I'm sure to you and everybody else it must appear that way, but it's what I felt I needed to do."

"Are you working somewhere else?"

"Not yet. I had some money saved, and I'm not going to rush into anything. Listen, Joe, I know none of this makes sense. I'm hoping one day it will; but for now, just be my friend and don't ask a lot of questions. We can discuss this further when we see each other. I really don't want to talk about it now."

"Speaking of which, that's one of the things I wanted to talk to you about. Seeing I just got back to Colorado Springs last night, I need to be in the office a few days; but I thought if you were free this weekend, I'd drive over to Grand Junction and maybe we could have dinner Saturday night. We could even hike the Monument Sunday morning before I head back."

Stan must not have told him that I left Colorado. How am I going to explain that I'm not in Grand Junction and that I'm leasing a condo in Sedona, Arizona? "Joe, I would love to see you and have dinner Saturday night, but unfortunately I can't."

"I should've known you'd have a hot date. I've been out of the country a long time—longer than I realized—and it's been a while since we talked. I had no idea you were even thinking of leaving the paper—never saw that one coming." The disappointment in his voice was obvious.

Kelly thought about her friendship with Joe and how important he'd become to her ... especially since Tara's death. The last time they were together, she sensed that if it wasn't for the three hundred miles separating them, he'd like for their friendship to progress further. She wanted Joe in her life, but with each of them living in different cities, she felt it best to keep their relationship platonic, and she didn't think she was ready to be in a committed relationship.

"First of all, I don't have a hot date. I would love to see you and catch up with what's been happening the last couple of months, but ..." she paused.

"But what?"

"Dang! I don't know how else to tell you, so I'll just blurt it out. Joe, I'm not in Grand Junction. I'm living in Sedona, Arizona—at least for the next six months, according to my lease." There was a disquieting silence on the other end. "Joe?"

"Give me a minute, Kelly. I know I'm tired. Actually, I'm exhausted. If I'm to understand you correctly, you're telling me that you walked away from a career you've put your heart and soul into and moved from a city that you said you didn't think you would ever leave. If this is true, you've either lost your mind or you really *are* sick. And just for the record, am I the last to know?"

Before she had time to answer, she was interrupted by the ringing of her doorbell. "Joe, someone's at my door. I haven't met anyone since I've been here so I can't imagine who it is. This shouldn't take long. Do you want to hold, or would you rather I call you back?"

"You go ahead. I've got a lot to do—haven't even unpacked yet. I'll catch up with you later in the week, bye, Kelly." He sounded annoyed and hung up abruptly. She hated to end the call that way, but she also felt grateful for the extra time to come up with a plausible explanation as to why she left her career and Colorado to reside in Sedona.

Chapter Four

"Hello, is anyone in there?" mumbled the young woman as she continued to ring the doorbell.

"I'm coming," Kelly called out, feeling irritated by the time she opened the door.

"Hi, I'm Gina. I live in one of the units over there," said the tall, thirty-something, curvaceous blond pointing across the parking lot to a condo complex. "I'm sorry to be persistent, but I keep missing you. I've stopped by numerous times to invite you to our neighborhood potluck—neighborhood meaning your condo complex and mine. In the last few weeks, we've had a lot of new tenants move in, so several of us got together and thought it would be a great opportunity to meet some new faces and help the newcomers feel welcome." The pretty blond extended her hand. "Welcome! My last name is Sanders! Gina Sanders. I've only been here six months, but I feel that it's home. I love Sedona!"

"Hi, Gina. I'm Kelly! Kelly Murphy. It's very nice to meet you. Thank you for the invitation, but since I don't plan on being here long-term, I probably shouldn't go. I'm only leasing for six months."

"I haven't been here that long either, Kelly. I've met several residents who've been here for years, but I've also met many who are only staying a few months. I've noticed that most people are friendly and seem to enjoy knowing their neighbors—even if only for a short time." She looked past Kelly into the living room and noticed the view off the balcony. "Wow! Aren't you lucky! What a fantastic view of Bell Rock. I would have chosen this building when I was looking for a place, but at the time, there weren't any units available."

Kelly opened the door wide and motioned for Gina to come in. "Let's continue our conversation inside ... that is, if you have the time."

"I do, and I would love to come in. Thank you." Gina walked through the living room straight to the sliding doors that led to the balcony.

"Go on out and make yourself comfortable. I'll get us something to drink."

"Water's fine for me, Thanks."

Kelly returned with two bottles of water and handed one to Gina. They both sat down at the patio table. "You'll have to excuse my appearance," Kelly said, looking down at her tattered shorts and T-shirt. "I decided to go for a hike before showering and putting on make-up. I obviously wasn't expecting to see anyone."

Gina, dressed in black slacks and an emerald-green, button-down blouse with a ruffled collar, could tell that Kelly felt self-conscious. "You're fine. I only look like this when I have a showing at the gallery. Most of the time, depending on the weather, I'm either in shorts and a T-shirt or jeans with a shirt or sweater."

"So, you're an artist? I'm impressed."

"That's not what I do for a living, though. If it was, I'd starve to death. It's just my hobby, but it helps me stay creative and keeps me in tune with my intuitive side. Once a year, the gallery where I'm showing today allows novice artists to display some of their work. The owner feels that it provides an inexpensive way for everyone to own a piece of artwork. It also helps the owner of this unique gallery to discover new talent. I'm always amazed at how good some of these unknown local artists really are."

"What a great opportunity! But if you don't make your living from your artwork, what exactly do you do here in Sedona—if you don't mind my asking?"

Gina smiled. "Not at all, Kelly. I hope you won't hold it against me," she took a swallow of her water and then continued, "but I'm actually a clairvoyant and I do readings at one of the psychic centers. I guess you've noticed that Sedona has quite a few of them—psychic centers, that is."

"Interesting," Kelly responded, slowly nodding her head.

Gina watched Kelly shift in her chair. She could tell that she'd become a little uneasy. "Relax! I'm not going to put a hex on you," she laughed in an attempt to make Kelly feel more comfortable. "Unfortunately, carnival fortune tellers—and the media, for the most part—have portrayed us sitting in front of a crystal ball performing magical hocus-pocus. Believe me, someone like myself who's been blessed with the gift of discernment would never tell anyone something that she didn't believe to be the truth."

"How can you be sure that what you're telling someone *is* the truth? Don't you worry about giving them information that could be harmful, or at best move them in the wrong direction?" Kelly asked with genuine interest.

Gina sipped her water, glanced momentarily at Bell Rock, and then began to explain her views. "When I first started doing readings, I did wonder if what I was saying could be influenced somewhat by my own bias and thoughts about things. So I was very careful about what I said. Over time, the more I learned to trust myself, the more I realized that when I sensed something strongly—especially if it came to me immediately—then I needed to tell my client. If what's coming to me is more vague, I also share that information and explain that it's what I'm feeling, but it isn't very clear to me. I've never intentionally misled anyone." She noticed the skeptical expression on Kelly's face. "Kelly, we all have intuition, but for some of us it's magnified—a sixth sense if you will—possibly heightened by a Higher Power. I'm also a very spiritual person, and I feel that my keen sense of knowing is a gift that I'm supposed to use to help others." She watched as Kelly fidgeted with her water bottle.

"I'll say one more thing, and then I promise to change subjects before you ask me to leave," she teased.

"I can tell I'm making you a little uncomfortable with what I'm saying, but I think it has more to do with being in denial about your own intuitive side than it does with me."

Kelly swallowed the rest of her water and acted nonchalant as though Gina's words weren't meant for her. "Would you like more water, Gina?" she asked.

"I'm fine for now. Kelly, once you get to know me, you'll realize that I'm no different than anyone else. Okay, enough about me. I'd like to know what *you* do for a living and what brings you here?"

"I'm surprised you don't already know," Kelly said with a chuckle.

Gina laughed. "Given what I've told you, I don't blame you for thinking that, but that's not the way it works. When I'm visiting someone, I'm not thinking about, or trying to sense, anything. If I were a psychiatrist, I don't suspect I'd be evaluating everyone I met. But if you'd like for me to do a reading, I can shift gears."

"No, thank you."

"Then please let your guard down and tell me about yourself."

Kelly smiled and relaxed her shoulders. "I'm sorry if I seem uptight, but it's been a crazy couple of months. I'm a journalist—uh, *was* a journalist. I'm not sure what I am anymore." Kelly went on to explain a little more about her own background and indicated that she wasn't really sure why she ended up in Sedona. They talked for another thirty minutes before Gina had to leave.

"I'm glad to have met you, Kelly. Maybe we can meet for lunch sometime and I can share what little I've learned about Sedona."

"That sounds good. It was nice meeting you too, Gina."

Before leaving, Gina left Kelly with a few thoughts to ponder. "Life can be a mystery, Kelly, but if we're open to the lessons we're supposed to learn while on this journey, we'll understand our purpose. Some people never follow their instincts and are always in conflict with what they should be doing. For whatever reason, and however long, I believe you're meant to be here."

"Are you saying you think there are lessons here that I need to learn?"

"Maybe. But it could also be that your presence here might benefit someone else. Just be open-minded to whatever comes your way, and trust your intuition."

Chapter Five

As she thought about Gina and how warm and friendly she was, Kelly was glad she'd asked her to come in. *I guess I can overlook the fact that Gina thinks she's gifted in ESP,* she thought, *and feels she has the right to advise others.*

After making a pot of coffee, she took a cup out on the balcony and deeply breathed the fresh morning air, which was beginning to heat up—typical for June. She leaned over the railing and inspected the field behind her, hoping to get a glimpse of wildlife. A few days earlier, just as the sun was setting, she'd seen two javelina come from the woods and cross the field to the unit below where they helped themselves to her neighbor's potted plants and cactus surrounding the patio. She'd heard of javelina when she first moved to Sedona, and even though they looked like wild pigs, she learned that they are actually members of the peccary family, a group of hoofed mammals originating from South America. She also learned that javelina are common in much of central and southern Arizona, but they've also been seen as far north as Flagstaff.

Her phone began to ring as she took her last sip of coffee. Staring at the unfamiliar number on her cell, Kelly stepped inside to refill her coffee and answered just before the call went to voice mail.

"Hello?"

"I'm looking for Kelly Murphy. Are you Kelly?" the stranger on the other end asked.

"I might be. To whom am I speaking?"

"This is Dan Mathews, an acquaintance of Joe Conrad's. He suggested I give you a call."

"Joe? Why would he ask you to call me?" she asked in disbelief, then wondered if something was wrong. She thought about how exhausted he was from his trip— how surprised and disappointed he sounded to learn that not only had she left her job and moved to Sedona, but she did it during the time he was out of the country trying to rescue a kidnapped child.

"By your response, I take it that you *are* Kelly Murphy."

"Yes, I am. Is Joe okay?"

"Oh yeah, he's fine, just busy playing catch-up after being out of the office for so long. I talked to him not more than ten minutes ago and your name came up."

Kelly didn't remember his name being mentioned in any of her conversations with Joe. "Are you working with Joe?"

"I don't work in Joe's office, but I have done some work for him. I'm a private investigator specializing in background checks and investigative research. Joe, like many other PIs, uses me, or my staff and the services I provide when they need a little more help and don't have the time to do the legwork and research. He called today to let me know that he was back in town and to thank me for my help on his last case. During the course of our conversation, your name came up when I mentioned that I'd be losing a key person at the end of the month and I was in a quandary as to how I'd ever replace him. Joe told me a little of your background. I understand that you were an investigative reporter with your local newspaper, but now you might be seeking other employment."

"Joe ... referred *me?*"

"Highly."

"Mr. Mathews ..."

"Please, Dan will do," he interrupted.

"Dan, I'm not a private investigator, and I've never worked for the police department, and I don't have any background in criminal law. I'm a reporter who used to work for a newspaper. My degree is in journalism. I don't believe I'd have the knowledge or expertise to do what you're looking for. Besides, even if I did, I'm not living in Colorado right now."

"I know. Neither am I. Although I seem to be on the road more than not, my office is in Flagstaff, Arizona, which isn't that far from Sedona."

Surprised, and wondering why Joe would have recommended her, Kelly momentarily forgot about the phone attached to her ear. She walked back out on the balcony and sat in the chair directly facing Bell Rock, leaving Dan Mathews to question if their connection had been lost.

"Hello? Are you still there?"

"Ah ... yes, Dan, I'm here. Did you say you were in Flagstaff?"

"That's correct. I suppose I should have waited to call until Joe had a chance to talk to you first. He said he'd be calling you shortly. I guess I jumped the gun. Now that I've explained the nature of my call, maybe you'd indulge my enthusiasm and meet with me at my office. You can see my mode of operation, meet my staff, and let me show you why I feel—based on talking with Joe—that you'd be a tremendous asset."

Kelly had to admit she was intrigued with the prospect of being in a working environment again, but she had her doubts. "I'm flattered to be considered for the position with your firm, and while it sounds very interesting, I need to mull all this over before I even commit to an appointment."

"That's understandable. Thanks to Joe, I was prepared for your response. He must know you pretty well. I hope he's as accurate with the rest of his prediction."

"And what might that be?" Kelly asked, feeling annoyed that Joe thought he knew how she'd react.

"Only that your sense of curiosity would move you to at least meet with me and find out what it is I actually do. I hope he's right, and maybe after talking with him, you'll feel better about the idea. Although I'm sure he won't expound on my virtues as he did with me about yours."

A smile came over Kelly's face. She thanked Dan for the call and assured him that she'd be in touch.

Chapter Six

Two days had passed since Dan Mathews' phone call, and Kelly still hadn't heard from Joe. *He must really be upset with me. I wonder if he even knows that I've spoken with Dan. Maybe I should call him.* She picked up her cell, but after she pressed his number in, she immediately pushed End. *What will I say to him? I know he's disappointed, maybe feeling hurt, and probably still a bit angry that I never told him about my plans. I did think about telling him but at the time it didn't seem like a good idea.* Kelly continued to rationalize her decision. *It didn't feel right to concern him with my problems while he was traversing around foreign countries hoping to safely return a stolen child to his family. He had enough on his plate. And besides, we only talked once, maybe twice at the most, during the entire time that he was out of the country.* The more she thought about it, the less sympathetic she felt towards Joe. *Why am I doing this? I shouldn't have to give him an explanation. It's not like we're a couple. We're friends and that's all! Friends who haven't been in touch for a while. I should be upset with him for not letting me know that I'd be hearing from Dan Mathews ...*

... Hmm, Dan Mathews. I wonder if I should set up an appointment with him. I guess it wouldn't hurt to see his place of

business, meet his staff, and have him explain in person exactly what the job entails. Besides, I can only hike for so long. I really do need something to do. Resting her phone on the coffee table, she went into the kitchen and opened the fridge. On the top shelf stood two bottles of water, a can of club soda and leftover salad from the night before. Two vanilla yogurts took space on the second shelf, along with an apple and an orange. She shook her head and decided she'd better jump in the shower before heading to the grocery store. As she passed by her phone on the way to the bedroom, it began to ring. Her first inclination was to ignore it and retrieve the message after she had showered and dressed. But as usual, Kelly had a hard time not answering a ringing phone. She hesitated when she saw Joe's name, but only for a moment.

"Hi, Joe," she said softly, slowly seating herself into the corner of the sofa.

"Kelly, sorry it's taken me a while to get back with you," he said in a matter-of-fact tone. "I talked to Dan Mathews yesterday, and I understand the two of you have spoken. I'm sure you must have questions, and you're probably wondering why I didn't let you know that he'd be calling."

Kelly was taken aback by the cordial indifference in Joe's voice. He didn't sound like the same Joe she'd gotten to know in Cripple Creek. He didn't sound like the person who helped her prove that Tara had been murdered and didn't accidentally fall off a cliff while hiking. And he certainly didn't sound like the man who came to her rescue when Tara's murderer also tried to kill her. She felt sad and regretful that she hadn't told him about her plans to leave the newspaper and move to Sedona.

"I *did* expect to hear from you," she said, but she wasn't thinking in reference to Dan Mathews. She'd hoped to get a call from Joe saying that while he didn't understand the decisions she'd made, she was his friend and he'd be supportive.

"Like I said when we talked last, I've been out of the country a long time, and I had a lot of catching up to do. I've really been busy this past week, but I'm sorry that I didn't call you before Dan did. Ask me whatever you want to know, and then I'll tell you why I felt Dan would be a good person for you to work with."

Joe obviously intended on keeping the conversation neutral and focused on Dan. *That's fine,* thought Kelly. *At least now I won't have to get defensive trying to explain my choices the last couple of months.* "Let's start with why you felt it was okay to discuss me with Dan in the first place, and why you felt the need to help me find a job when I clearly hadn't indicated that I was even in the market for one." These were not the questions Kelly had planned to ask him, and she was surprised by them and at how annoyed she sounded. She was more hurt by Joe's indifference than she realized, but she didn't want him to know it, and she didn't want to make matters more strained than what they already were. "I didn't mean for that to come out the way it did. It just felt uncomfortable being talked about to someone I didn't know. Maybe if I were seeking employment it wouldn't have bothered me."

"This is not working!" Joe blurted.

"Excuse me?"

"Kelly, I have questions of my own. I thought I could brush them aside, pretend they didn't bother me, and deal with them later, but unfortunately I can't. I can tell we're both on edge, and I don't want it to be this way. Listen, I'm planning on being in Flagstaff the first of the week. Dan and I have been trying to get together way before I even started on the kidnapping case. I didn't plan on seeing you when I visited Dan, but I think it might be a good idea. I'd like to see you, and I'd like to try and understand where your head is right now—that is, if you're willing to see *me*."

Her emotions conflicted like a mini tornado swirling within her at the thought of seeing Joe in a few days. Since arriving in Sedona, she'd tried to keep herself busy by hiking, going to the multitude of art galleries in the area, and even taking in a UFO tour one evening. But she knew the time would come when she'd have to evaluate the cost of leaving her job and Colorado, and what she was going to do next. She wondered if the butterflies in her stomach were a result of Joe wanting to see her or from knowing that his visit would no doubt cause her to face what she'd been putting off for too long.

Chapter Seven

First thing Monday morning, Joe called his office and checked with Betty, his secretary, to make sure his week had been cleared. Ever since becoming a private investigator Joe always worked alone, and he never felt the need for someone to run his office—until his last two cases, that is. Prior to the kidnapping case, he was involved with helping his former police department solve a ten-year-old cold case, and he spent more time in New Mexico tracking down leads than he did in Colorado. When he returned, he realized that he, and his office, could use some help, if for no other reason than to answer the phone and sort through mail. It was time to hire a secretary so he placed an ad in the Colorado Springs newspaper. When Betty walked in on the very first day that the ad ran, he knew he'd hit payday. She had been a legal secretary for one of the larger law firms in Colorado Springs, but when two of the owners retired within months of each other, her services were no longer needed. Joe found Betty to be bright, direct, and very pleasant. She'd been widowed for two years and had two married children, a son and a daughter, but no grandchildren yet. When she told Joe that she could be available to work nights and even weekends if he needed her, he knew she was the one. He was hoping to find someone with no strings attached, and he was sure Betty would be a perfect fit.

Most of Joe's friends and close acquaintances had access to his cell number, but it was a tremendous help to have Betty filter the rest of his calls. She kept everything in the office neat and organized, including herself. She took pride in keeping her plump form well-dressed. And her short, dark-brown hair adorned with blond highlights always looked as though she'd just stepped out of the salon. No sooner had he hung up from checking in with Betty when his phone rang. "Hey, Dan. You were the next on my call list. I'm flying out this afternoon. I would have called last night, but I didn't have everything firmed up until late."

"I knew you said you'd try to leave today and be in my office tomorrow morning, but I thought I'd better call and see if you needed someone to pick you up at the airport, and if you had a room yet."

"Thanks, Dan, but I'm all set. Betty has me staying at the Holiday Inn not far from your office, and she's made arrangements for a rental car at the airport."

"Joe, have you talked to Kelly Murphy? I don't want to seem pushy, but I haven't heard back from her, and I'd like to know if she's at least thinking about meeting with me."

"Yes, I was just getting ready to tell you about it. I spoke with her over the weekend, and as it turns out, I'll be seeing her tonight. She said she wanted to wait until after we met and had a chance to talk with me a little more about the position, and about you. She'll give you a call tomorrow."

"Hope I'm not wasting my time."

"Believe me, Dan, you're not. If Kelly was still in Colorado, *I'd* be hiring her. She won't let you down."

"Okay, I'll trust your judgment. I'd better let you go so you can pack and get to the airport on time. See you first thing in the morning. Have a safe trip."

"Thanks. I'll be there when the doors open at nine a.m. Bye now."

As Joe packed, he couldn't help thinking about Kelly. He was still upset with her for leaving Colorado and not telling him, but he felt a twinge of excitement at the thought of seeing her again. He wondered how the evening would go. He thought about his remark to Dan, that if she was still in Colorado he'd be hiring her. He held the last shirt to be placed in the suitcase and paused when it hit him that maybe one of the reasons he felt disappointed and frustrated with Kelly was that he missed his opportunity.

Chapter Eight

After straightening up the condo and making a list of hors d'oeuvres she thought Joe would like, Kelly was running out of things to do to distract her from the antsy jitters she was feeling. When they decided to meet at her place Monday night, Kelly offered to make dinner for Joe, but he insisted that she not go to the trouble, stating that if his flight was delayed he'd hate to ruin a good meal. She persuaded him to at least accept drinks and hors d'oeuvres since they could be refrigerated until he arrived.

She'd thought of Joe all day and wondered how it would feel to see him again. Months had passed since his last visit to Grand Junction, and she fondly remembered how the day went. He arrived late on a Friday night, so they agreed to meet Saturday morning for breakfast and then go for a hike on the Colorado National Monument. When they came to the exact spot where Tara had lost her life—after being pushed off the cliff—Kelly paused and knelt down. Placing a handful of wildflowers next to a rock, she spoke softly as if Tara could hear her. Now that the killer was dead, and Tara's death was finally ruled a homicide, she felt Tara was at peace.

There were many times since the tragedy that Kelly had come to the Monument to visit her friend, but on that day when Joe was with her, she felt Tara's presence just as she had at the funeral. A calming, comforting sensation went through her.

As Kelly prepared for the evening, she hoped she and Joe could get back to the friendship that had meant so much to her. She cared a lot for Joe, but she didn't want to become involved romantically because she wasn't ready emotionally for that kind of commitment. She preferred to keep it simple with no strings attached, but she was discovering that even friendships can get complicated.

I have nothing to give to move this friendship forward right now. I mean, I can't even figure out why I'm in a condo in Sedona, she thought. *I wish I understood why I've been so restless the last few months, and why I experienced such an overwhelming feeling that I needed to be elsewhere other than at my job in Colorado. Maybe I need to see a psychiatrist. Maybe she'd tell me that—considering what I went through when my best friend was murdered, and then almost losing my own life—it's not unusual to want to move on ... even if it means changing my surroundings. Whatever's going on with me, I'm sure it will become evident soon enough,* she thought. *For now, I have to put it to rest and hope that Joe doesn't bombard me with questions. I just want this evening to start off on the right foot.*

Kelly didn't expect Joe to arrive much before seven, but she'd already showered, put on some light make-up, and donned a paisley sundress that complimented her fair skin and brought out the green in her eyes. She was ready but still had a couple of hours to wait, so she sat on the sofa and put on the TV. The door bell rang just as the news got underway. *That can't be Joe. It's only five o'clock.* She was surprised to see Gina when she opened the door.

"Hi, Kelly. Gee, you look great! Sorry if I'm intruding." She looked past Kelly to see if anyone was inside "Are you on your way out?" she asked.

"No, I have a friend coming over later." She noticed Gina staring at her in disbelief. "I guess I do look a little more presentable from when we first met."

Gina laughed. "There was nothing wrong with your appearance the other day, but I must admit, I was expecting to see you in shorts, a T-shirt, and your hair pulled back in a ponytail. But I like your hair hanging down on your shoulders. It really shows off your beautiful, dark-auburn tones and the green in your eyes. Kelly, since you're expecting company, I won't take up your time. I mainly came over to give you my phone number. Being new to Sedona, I thought it might be nice for you to have someone to call should you need information about anything."

"Thank you, Gina. I really appreciate it." She held the door open and asked her to come inside, assuring her that she had the time. She turned off the TV and went to get her phone, which contained her contact numbers and addresses. She told Gina that if she didn't put it in its proper place, she'd lose it for sure.

Gina wrote down her email address in addition to her phone number. "I use this number for my landline, too. I don't see the need to have both. My phone is with me at all times, and now that I have a smart phone, I check my email on it more than I do on my computer."

"I feel the same way," Kelly said. She felt very comfortable with Gina and reciprocated with her own phone number and email address. Kelly was trusting by nature, but having been a reporter for over a decade, she had become more reserved and skeptical when first meeting someone. She felt it refreshing to instinctively be at ease around Gina.

"Well, I thank you much," said Gina, "but I'd better be leaving now before your friend arrives. Oh, I almost forgot, I wanted to ask if you'd given any thought about coming to our neighborhood potluck."

"Gina, please stay for a while. He won't be here until seven at the earliest. I haven't made up my mind about the potluck, but I probably will come."

"He? I should have known. See, I told you: When I'm not in the 'reading-people' mode, I know nothing," Gina said with a smile.

"It's not what you think. We're just friends, but I haven't seen him for a while ..."

Gina broke in. "You're worried about how you'll reconnect, aren't you? Don't be, the evening will go fine. But Kelly, if you ask me, the fact that you're concerned about it tells me there's more going on here than a casual friendship."

Kelly squinted her eyes and curled up her nose. "I thought you said your reading mode was off."

"It is. What I'm telling you is nothing more than a woman-to-woman, friend-to-friend observation. Let your guard down and be yourself. I repeat, the evening will go fine."

"We'll see."

Chapter Nine

Joe arrived a little after seven with a bouquet of flowers in one hand and a bottle of champagne in the other. "I come bearing gifts, hoping to ward off any ill will," he said when Kelly opened the door. She laughed and let him in. He handed her the flowers and gave her a hug. It felt like old times, and she hoped Gina was right: The evening would go fine.

Over brie and champagne they kept the conversation light, talking about the weather and what a hot summer both Colorado and Arizona were having. Kelly asked about Betty and if hiring a secretary proved to be fruitful. Joe beamed when he expounded on Betty's virtues. He said he didn't know how he would have managed without her during the time he was out of the country. Trying to keep the conversation away from herself, Kelly asked him to share what he could about the kidnapping case. When that subject was exhausted, she had one topic left, which she hoped would take up the rest of the evening, leaving the discussion of her situation for another time.

"I'm glad you could come over this evening," she said, offering another round of smoked salmon and brie. "It's good to see you, and I'm glad that you're no worse for wear from your travels." She tried to be discreet and not stare at him, but she couldn't help notice how handsome he looked. It appeared his tall well-built frame had not gained an ounce. She thought she saw a few more strands of grey in his thick dark hair, and maybe a few sprigs in his mustache, but she felt it only added to his charm and character. *I think now would be a good time to talk about Dan Mathews,* she thought.

"I definitely want to talk with you about Dan," Joe began, almost as if reading her mind, "but I was hoping we could discuss *you* first." He finally brought up the subject she dreaded. "I've thought a lot about this while I was on the plane and during the drive over here," he continued. Kelly bristled, anticipating what was going to come next, but to her surprise, he was very compassionate. "I'm not going to pretend that I can understand what you're doing here," he shook his head and grinned. "Hell, Kelly, I've always had trouble understanding *you,* but maybe that's what makes you so interesting."

Kelly chuckled. Now that she was more relaxed, she leaned back into the fold of the sofa and sipped her champagne. "Well, Joe, at least you're not alone—in understanding me, that is. I haven't been able to do that for some time now." She looked straight ahead through the sliding doors and noticed the full moon. Downing the last sip of her champagne, she set her glass on the table and turned to Joe. "It's late enough now to be comfortable on the patio. There might even be a breeze. Would you like to sit out there and have a brandy?"

"Is this your way of avoiding the subject?"

"No, not at all—at least I don't think so—but I'm not sure that I have any satisfactory answers for you. I'm still trying to sort through it all myself. Why don't you go out and I'll fix the brandy." When she started to get up, Joe grabbed her hand.

"Please, wait a minute. I have something I want to say first." Curious, she sat back down. "Like I said, I've thought a lot about this. I might not be the most sensitive guy in the world, but eventually some things do register with me." Still holding her hand, he looked into her eyes and continued. "Kelly, you've lost a lot of people in your life within a short amount of time—your father, your mother, Tara—and you almost lost your own life. I don't know if you've taken the time to fully grieve for each of them. Maybe you have, but something else occurred to me on the drive over here, and I don't believe you've worked through it."

Kelly didn't know where Joe was going with all this, and she wasn't sure she wanted to hear any more. "Let me get the brandy and we can go out on the patio. I think I'd like some fresh air."

He ignored her and continued. "I remembered you telling me that the day of Tara's death, she had asked you to go hiking with her, but you were busy so you declined. I believe you're still carrying guilt for not being with her, and I believe you still think if you *had* gone hiking with her, she'd be alive today."

Kelly's eyes filled, and she gently pulled her hand away from Joe's and shook her head. "I'll always carry guilt for not being with her, but I've felt Tara on many occasions, and I know she wouldn't want me to dwell on this, so I try not to. I don't think it has anything to do with why I'm in Sedona."

"Maybe not. But considering the fact that you survived your own brutal attack and Tara didn't caused me to wonder if you might be suffering from survivors' remorse. I considered that this, along with the fact that Tara's been gone a year now, might be the catalyst that drove you to leave the life you knew." There was a pause where they were both quiet. "Anyway, thinking about it this way helped me to gain a different perspective. I can't judge why you did what you did, or feel sorry for myself because you didn't confide in me. I'm not in your shoes, and I don't know what you're going through." He took her hand again and squeezed it. "What I've come to realize is, while I may not understand your drastic measures—any more than you do at this point—I'm your friend and I want to help you through this."

Kelly teared up even more, but it wasn't only because of the painful memories Joe had brought up—she'd certainly given thought to all of that over the past few weeks—but it had more to do with how lonely she'd been since leaving Stan and the *Sentinel*, which had been her life for so long. And she now felt even more grateful for her friendship with Joe.

"Joe, I appreciate your support and concern. Your thoughts are valid, but while I may not know for sure the reason I'm here, I don't feel it has anything to do with Tara or anything else in my past. I may not understand it right now, but there's one thing I do know and feel with every cell in my body, and that is that I'm supposed to be here. Thank you for trying to understand, and for being my friend. I need that more than anything right now."

He smiled and gently brushed away the tear in the corner of her eye and helped her up. "Maybe you're right, Kelly, we'll just have to wait and see. I'll help you with the brandy and we can discuss Dan while we sip it on the patio. Who knows? If you're supposed to be here, then maybe you're meant to work with Dan Mathews."

Chapter Ten

When Joe arrived, he noticed that Dan already had someone in his office. It wasn't unusual for people to drop in without an appointment but, on most occasions, Dan wouldn't be there and they'd be directed to one of his associates. Dan wasn't a pretentious person, and he liked his surroundings to be kept simple. His office was of a comfortable size with glass walls facing the entrance. He liked seeing into the atrium, but he also had blinds to pull when privacy was desired. He saw Joe in the lobby and waved to him. Joe nodded and motioned for him not to hurry. He took a seat in front of a round glass coffee table and grabbed a magazine. No one was behind the receptionist's desk, but Joe had arrived early knowing that Dan would be there. Ten minutes passed before the two men came out of Dan's office. Dan walked the young man to the door, thanked him for coming, and assured him that he'd be in touch within the next two days. Then he walked over to Joe and extended his hand.

"Good to see you! Sorry for the wait."

"No problem. I knew I was a little early."

"Let's go in my office. I'm anxious to talk to you."

Joe followed him and took the chair in front of Dan's desk.

"Did you see Kelly last night?"

"Yes, I did."

"Did you talk to her about the position?"

"Geez, Dan, you don't waste any time. Is that the most pressing thing on your mind this morning?"

"As a matter of fact, it is. News travels fast around here. The guy who was just here heard I had an opening and stopped by to apply. He may be young, but he's licensed and pretty sharp. This Kelly friend of yours isn't a licensed private investigator—which, I realize, isn't required in Colorado—but still, she never worked as an investigator when she was living there. Joe, I'm not sure why you're so insistent that I interview her."

"Trust me, she's a natural. What she lacks in training, she makes up for with her instincts. Kelly's a quick study and will learn whatever she needs to, but instincts can't be taught—you either have it or you don't. And I'm telling you, she's got it."

"That's what I want to hear, and that's what I've been waiting for. You know, Joe, you and I rely a lot on our gut feeling, but it's taken years of experience to trust it. I worked beside Tom for many years and, to be honest, I doubt that I'll ever be able to replace him. We were in sync with everything we did, and we could even pick up on each other's thoughts without having to explain every detail. But I knew this day would come. Tom's been talking about retiring for a long time, and I wasn't prepared for how much I'd miss working with him."

"I understand what you're saying, and that's why I think you should take the time to talk with Kelly."

Dan glanced around his office and took a deep breath. "It's taken me years to build what I have here," he said, looking directly at Joe. "My reputation is the only thing I give a damn about when I leave this world. I want my family to walk around town with their heads held high, knowing their father, husband, brother, and uncle was a well-respected and trusted individual. Hell, Joe, I'm going to be seventy next month," he said, rubbing his balding head and patting his bulging stomach.

Joe shook his head in disbelief. "I never would have guessed you were almost seventy! You can still do circles around anyone, including me. I don't know where you get your energy."

"Never seriously thought about retiring until Tom did. Joan and I have talked about it a lot since. She's always wanted to travel, and I've always been too busy. I'd like to work another five to ten years, but I made a promise to her last week that I'd ease up a little so we can take a trip now and then, and she can see all the places she's been missing. I won't be able to do that unless I can get someone in here who I trust. Tom and I made Brad a junior partner a few years ago, and he's great at what he does, but he doesn't have the time to babysit someone new. I rely on him completely, as I do the rest of my staff, and I need to trust and depend on whoever else I bring on board."

"I couldn't agree more, and that's why you should talk to Kelly. Let's give her a call and get her in here."

Chapter Eleven

Sipping coffee and checking her emails, Kelly was interrupted by the doorbell. She couldn't imagine who would be stopping by at eight in the morning.

"Gina?"

"Hi, Kelly. I'm on my way to the center. I have five readings scheduled for today, but I wanted to stop by and give you a welcoming gift." She handed Kelly a large flat item wrapped in brown packing paper. "Go ahead and open it. I want to see your reaction before I leave." Still standing in the doorway, Kelly tore apart the loose-fitting wrapper. She was speechless when she saw what it was.

"I started it weeks ago," said Gina, "but the first time I was over here sitting out on your balcony, I knew it belonged to you. While it may not be the best painting of Bell Rock, I thought it turned out pretty good. What do you think of it?"

Kelly couldn't take her eyes off it. She was mesmerized by how realistic the painting looked. "It's beautiful, Gina! Absolutely beautiful! The colors are so true, and the detail—wow! I can even see the area where I hike." She looked at Gina. "I don't know how to thank you. I've never received such a thoughtful gift in my life. Gina, you're really good! How can you call yourself a novice artist? You're much better than that!"

"Thanks, Kelly! I'm so glad you like it. Wish I could come in and help you find the perfect place to hang it, but if I don't leave now, I'll be late. Catch you later."

Kelly closed the door and went over to the sofa. Holding the painting with both hands, she admired the beautiful detail Gina had put into it. As she continued to study every inch of Bell Rock, the hiking paths, and all the foliage Gina had captured, her heart skipped a beat when she came across a juniper tree off a familiar path.

A little past nine, Kelly answered her phone, and wasn't surprised to hear Dan's voice on the other end. She knew Joe had a morning meeting with him, and he told her the night before that Dan would probably be calling her when they finished. But he didn't tell her to be ready to come to Dan's office as soon as she hung up.

Kelly sifted through the slim collection of hanging items in her bedroom closet, hoping to find an outfit presentable for an interview. When leaving Colorado, she'd packed plenty of casual clothing, but business attire was not a priority, especially since she didn't know what she'd be doing in Sedona. Becoming frustrated after sliding the hangers back and forth numerous times, she finally grabbed dark tan pants and a light-beige peasant blouse, then headed for a quick shower.

When she arrived at the office building, she was surprised to see that Joe was still there. He came over to greet her. "Good morning, Kelly. I'm glad you could make it on such short notice," he said, grinning from ear to ear.

"Morning, Joe ... what's left of it," she said, observing the clock on the wall. "I wasn't expecting to see you."

"I hope you don't mind. Dan and I were just shooting the breeze until you got here. Once you agreed to come in, I thought I'd hang around and introduce the two of you."

"Did you doubt I was capable of introducing myself?" she teased with a flare of sarcasm.

"Who *me*? Doubt *your* capabilities? Never!" he said, returning the sarcasm with a grin.

Kelly smiled, and then looked at the clock again. "We'd better not keep Dan waiting any longer."

"Right, especially since he can see us. He's probably wondering what lies I'm telling." Joe took her by the arm and escorted her into Dan's office, where he made the introductions. Smiling, Dan asked her to have a seat, and she took the chair that Joe had been sitting in. Joe pulled up another chair and placed it next to Kelly. Kelly stared at him as if to say, "What do you think you're doing?" Dan, noticing the situation, pretended to clear his throat.

"Oh, you're right. This is *your* interview and I'm sure you don't need my help." Kelly shot Joe another look that he understood all too well. Finally getting his cue to leave, he thanked Dan again for all his help over the last few months, and said he'd be in touch. He slowly moved between Kelly and the desk, blocking Dan's view.

In a whisper—which he hoped only she could hear—he relayed what had been on his mind since she'd walked through the door.

"Kelly, you look stunning!"

She blushed, squinted her eyes, and nodded her head toward the door for him to leave. He winked and gave her a big smile as he left.

Chapter Twelve

Dan wasted no time in his effort to learn more about Kelly. They talked a lot about her time with the *Sentinel*, and her editor and friend, Stan. He found her to be bright, humorous, and easy to talk with. She was everything Joe had said she was, and more. He felt very comfortable with her and shared some of his own experiences. He told her about a couple of cases he and Tom had worked on, and about the void Tom left when he retired.

Kelly listened with interest, but reiterated that—while she may have done some investigative reporting for her hometown newspaper—by no means did she have any experience as a private investigator. "It's obvious that you had a very special friendship and business relationship with your partner, Tom, and I'm not sure anyone could fill those shoes—least of all me," she said.

Dan leaned back in his chair, took off his glasses, and let them dangle from his hand while allowing her words to simmer a moment. Then he leaned forward, and put them back on, but they were resting lower on his nose as he stared at Kelly over the top of them. "You know something, Kelly? You're right. Those *are* very large shoes to fill. You know what else? You just helped me realize that I don't want to fill them, even though I think that's what I was hoping to do." He adjusted his glasses back on the bridge of his nose and relaxed back in his chair.

"I'm going to be retiring one of these days, possibly sooner than I'd anticipated. One never knows what circumstances might arise to cause a change of plans. I had a vision for this firm when that day came, but I'm not too sure that the direction I was leaning toward would have been the best after all. I really don't need another partner, especially since I'm not sure how much longer I'll be doing this. What I could use is a good assistant, someone with sound judgment. Kelly, with your background at the newspaper, I feel you'd be more than qualified. I have enough PIs in this office, and I believe Joe is right about you. I think you'd offer a different dimension."

"Thank you! I appreciate the confidence. And while it's tempting to rejoin the work force, do you have a clear picture of what I'd be doing?"

Dan chuckled. "If I'm to be honest, I don't know that I do; however, I do know that I need help, and I'm beginning to see where you might fit in. Maybe together we can define your position. I'd like to bring you onboard, Kelly. I hope you'll accept. We have a great working environment, and everyone here is like family. What do you say?" He noticed she was looking through the glass wall toward the reception desk. One of his coworkers was picking up messages. "That's

Evan. He's only been here for a year and a half, but he's doing a great job. The woman behind the desk is Ruth. She's a real sweetheart, and she's been with me for twenty years. I tease her and call her my little sis. Would you like to meet them, as well as the rest of our family?"

Kelly smiled. "I guess I did get distracted."

"It's easy to do with the glass walls," Dan acknowledged. "I could pull the drapes, if you'd like."

"Oh, no, not on my account. I like the openness that the glass walls give. It's as if you're saying, 'We have nothing to hide,' It reminds me of being at the newspaper with all the open cubicles." She smiled. "I like it, and I like the way you referred to your staff as 'family'—that feels familiar, too. I'd like to meet everyone, but I'll save that for another day—perhaps when I know for certain if I'll be working here."

"At least it sounds like you might be considering it. Why are you hesitant, if I may ask?"

"Being a journalist and working for the newspaper is all I've ever known. Working in a different field is not something I ever gave serious thought to, but I'm interested. I'd like a couple of days to mull it over so I can be fair to both of us. I wouldn't want to accept the position and then a few weeks later, feel that I'd made a mistake. Can you give me forty-eight hours to consider your offer? I don't expect you to stop interviewing, and I realize I risk the chance of someone else getting the position. But I need time to make sure that I'd be doing the right thing."

"I understand where you're coming from, and I don't think it's too much to ask. After all, you didn't call for an interview. I called you. There are a few other things we should probably discuss before you leave—like salary and benefits—knowing that that information might be helpful in making your decision."

"That won't be necessary, at least not until I know for sure what I'm going to do. Besides, I have a feeling that how I'm compensated won't be an issue." Smiling, she shook his hand and assured him that she'd be in touch soon.

Chapter Thirteen

Present Day

Her thoughts of the past few weeks cleared when she heard Joe at the door. Once he stepped inside, Kelly immediately began to describe her day in elaborate detail: finding the knife buried beneath the juniper tree, and how she was drawn to that very spot. Then she showed him the article about the woman from Jerome whose body was found at Bell Rock. "The article doesn't say how she died," Kelly began, "whether it was from a fall, strangulation, gunshot wound, or knife—only that it was a homicide."

"So, based on that article, you think the knife you found could be the murder weapon? Why would you think that?"

"Because it's not your typical picnic paring knife," she said in a frustrated tone. "Do you think I would have asked you to come over here if it were?"

"Of course not! I'm just trying to figure out what it was about the knife that freaked you out. Is it still in your backpack?"

"Yes, and it's going to stay there until we decide if I should call the police. I'll open the pack and show it to you, then you can tell me if it looks suspicious or not." She placed the bag on the coffee table in the living room. Joe settled himself on the sofa in front of it and Kelly sat next to him. When she opened the bag, Joe's eyes widened as he looked at the large knife with what appeared to be dried blood stains mixed with dirt and rotted pine needles.

"Geez, Kelly, that's not what I expected! Unless this was used on an animal, I'd say there's a good possibility you just might have found the murder weapon."

"Joe, there's something else I haven't told you."

"What's that?"

She told him about the stranger who stopped to rest on the rock across from her while she was meditating. "He seemed harmless enough, and we engaged in idle chitchat until other people came along, and then he left. It wasn't until I found the knife that I felt uneasy about him—actually, I was downright frightened." She proceeded to tell Joe how she had an eerie feeling that someone was watching her when she put the knife in her backpack. And when she turned around, she saw the same man, and he was moving toward her at a very fast pace until he saw several hikers coming down the path. Then he quickly left.

"Kelly, this is the investigator in me asking, and it's not meant to minimize what you've been through, but did he seem threatening, or maybe he was just interested in what you might have found?"

"At the time, I felt threatened. I don't know, Joe, I had just found what looked like a bloody butcher knife, and maybe that played into my feelings. But he didn't say a word, and he didn't smile. He just came right at me, and it scared me."

"I can see why. It bothers me that it happened. It may be a freak coincidence, but we need to take this seriously—at least until we know more."

"Now you see why I was concerned. I guess this is where I call the police?"

"Or the sheriff's office," said Joe. "You said the article mentioned a Sheriff Gardner. I passed a sheriff's vehicle as I was turning onto your street, but the police could also be involved. Sedona's a small place, and I don't know who has jurisdiction over the Bell Rock area, but I'll find out." He called the police department and learned that Bell Rock was in the county, so the sheriff would be the one to call.

Kelly blurted out her concerns about being questioned by the sheriff. "He's not going to believe I was drawn to that tree, and he's definitely not going to believe that I felt it was trying to tell me something. He'll either think I'm a lunatic or that I know more than what I'm telling him."

Joe smiled. "Relax, Kelly. You're in Sedona. This is the place where intuition and unusual feelings abound."

Kelly squinted her eyes and wrinkled her nose at him. "That may be, but the sheriff could think I might be involved in some way. If he doesn't buy the intuition aspect, then he might question why I would dig around a tree when all I saw was a little shiny spot. What if I become a person of interest?"

"Get a grip! Your imagination is running wild," Joe countered. "Let me put this in perspective: The young woman was murdered months before you arrived. There's no way you could have known anything. The article didn't say how she was murdered, only that it was a homicide. Maybe she was shot, or strangled. The knife could be completely unrelated to her murder. Yes, it does look suspicious, but it could have been buried there years before she died. And if it will make you feel more comfortable, you can always tell him you love trees and you were taking pictures when you noticed something shiny at the base of the juniper ... but then he'd probably want to see your camera," he added with a grin.

She sighed. "Seriously, Joe, I know I'm being ridiculous, but I haven't been in this predicament before, and being in a new area with nothing to do probably makes me a little paranoid. But as you said, I wasn't even in Sedona when that young woman was murdered, so ... I guess I'll go to the sheriff's office after we eat lunch. You have a plane to catch, and I can handle it from here. I just needed to talk to you about it." She gave him a big smile, and then she made her way to the refrigerator and took out the salad she'd fixed earlier.

"I hope you didn't go to too much trouble," Joe said, looking at a large bowl of food.

"Not at all. It's just a tossed salad with some leftover chicken I had for dinner last night."

During lunch, they continued to talk about the knife and if it could possibly be connected to the murdered woman at Bell Rock, speculating as to why someone would have wanted to kill her. "We'll start with the sheriff and see how much he'll tell us. Then I'll contact Dan and see what he can dig up on Melanie Davies. Maybe he's even heard something about the case. Speaking of Dan, how did your interview go?"

"I'm sure you've spoken with him, so why don't you tell me how *he* felt it went?"

"This may surprise you, Kelly, but I haven't talked to Dan since I was in his office," he winked, adding, "not that I didn't try, but he was on the other line. I left word I'd call him back when I got to Colorado Springs. I'm sure I know what Dan thought of you, but what did you think of him? Did he offer you the job and, if so, did you take it?"

"I like Dan. He seems honest and straightforward, and he probably would be a good person to work with. As a matter-of-fact, one of the reasons I went to Bell Rock this morning was to clear my head and give serious thought to the position Dan wants to fill. Something interesting happened during the course of our conversation. He realized when we were talking that maybe he didn't want someone to replace Tom. Instead, he decided what he really needs is an assistant, and that's the position I was offered." While she cleared the table, she continued to fill Joe in on her meeting with Dan.

Now that lunch was out of the way, there was only one thing left to do: Take the backpack to the sheriff.

Kelly stared at it with dread. "I guess I could wait until morning to take this, but I'm anxious to get it out of here. To be honest, my reporter curiosity wants to know more. Joe, I hope I haven't kept you too long. Oh gosh, I've been so preoccupied that I didn't even ask if you were able to get a later flight."

"I don't leave until tomorrow night. Unfortunately, that was the best they could do. I called Betty and had her get me a room close to here—didn't think you'd want me crashing on your sofa," he added, smiling.

"Oh, geez, I've really messed you up. Joe, I'm sorry. I don't know why this knife thing rattled me the way it did. I shouldn't have said anything until you were back in the Springs. You really don't need to stay in Sedona tonight. I certainly can handle this on my own." She felt foolish now for involving him.

"Well, I'm here, and I, too, am curious. Let's see what the sheriff has to say."

Chapter Fourteen

"Let me get this straight," said Sheriff Gardner. "You have a knife in your backpack that you found buried underneath a juniper tree at the base of Bell Rock. Correct?"

"Yes," Kelly said confidently. She fidgeted as she stood in front of the sheriff's desk.

"What is it about this knife that led you to believe it should be brought in?"

"Rather than try to explain, maybe it would be better if you look at the knife and determine for yourself whether it's suspicious or not. It looks to me as though there's blood on it," Kelly said as she carefully opened the backpack and gingerly pulled out the knife, holding it with a tissue. "I've tried not to disturb anything on the blade or the handle, should it prove to be important." She placed the knife on top of the towel she brought from home and laid it on Sheriff Gardner's desk. He was quick to respond.

"Well, I'll be damned!" he said, staring down at the object. "We have an unsolved homicide that took place on Bell Rock a while back. She was a young woman from Jerome, and she was stabbed multiple times with what was believed to be a butcher knife. The weapon was never found and we were never able to charge anyone," he said, studying the knife. Then he quickly turned his attention to Kelly. "That area was searched repeatedly for any sign of a weapon or clue that might have been left behind by whoever did it, but nothing was found. Where exactly did you find the knife?"

Kelly hesitated because she knew the knife was off the trail she usually took. "It's hard to pinpoint the exact spot. I guess I'd have to show you."

Standing beside her, Joe jumped in explaining how Kelly had called him when she'd returned from her hike and how rattled she was by finding the knife.

"And why would she call you?" asked the sheriff. Joe continued, talking about Dan, Kelly's interview, and why he was in Sedona. Joe told him about meeting Kelly in Cripple Creek when he was working on another case. He also told him about Tara.

"It hasn't been that long since Kelly almost lost her own life at the hands of Tara's murderer. I can only imagine how she felt when she found a blood-stained butcher knife while on a routine hike. Knowing I was still in the area, it made sense for her to call me."

"So you're a PI?" Sheriff Gardner asked with interest.

"Yup, and a former police detective." Joe told him about having worked with the Colorado Springs Police Department and then mentioned that Kelly was from Grand Junction, where she'd worked as a reporter. Kelly stood in silence, relieved that Joe was doing most of the talking.

The sheriff turned his attention back to Kelly. "And you're a newspaper reporter?"

"Was. I'm unemployed at the moment."

"But not for long, I hope," said Joe, glancing at Kelly.

"Yes, I'm considering an opportunity to work with Dan Mathews." Kelly decided it was about time she told him about the stranger. "Sheriff, there was something else that happened at Bell Rock that unnerved me." She told him about the man and how she had a sense that he might have been watching her. "I don't know if he actually saw me dig up the knife, but I'm reasonably sure that he watched me put something in my backpack."

"Ms. Murphy, I've known some people who believe you shouldn't disturb the earth or take anything like rocks, etc., from what's considered a spiritual place or vortex. Hell, they'll even come right up to you and make you drop it," said the sheriff, still eyeing the knife.

"Sheriff, the man told me he was from Nebraska. I don't think he was concerned with whether or not I was putting rocks in my backpack."

That got Sheriff Gardner's attention. "I see your point. So, tell me, what did this guy look like?"

Kelly described him as best she could—that he was tall and muscular, and how he was dressed. "Unfortunately, I didn't pay much attention to his face. The sun was in my eyes, and his red Huskers cap was pulled down on his forehead. He was also wearing sunglasses. That's all I can tell you. At the time, I was unaware of how useful the information could be."

"That's helpful," Sheriff Gardner said, as he wrote the description down.

"Do you know of any reports from other women claiming to be followed or seeing someone lurking nearby?" Kelly asked.

"Nothing's been brought to my attention, but I'll check over at the police department to see if they've had any complaints. But if this guy really is from Nebraska and only here for a visit, I don't know how he would've known Melanie Davies, or how he could have been involved—unless he's lying."

Studying the knife again, he motioned for Kelly and Joe to take a seat. "I'd like to think this knife is the murder weapon in the Davies case. The only way to find out is to send it to the Arizona Bureau of Investigation and have the lab check it out. Hopefully they'll find some DNA that will match the young woman's and that of the person who killed her." The sheriff ran his fingers through his thinning hair and shook his head. "I've been haunted by this case. Melanie Davies had no enemies, no skeletons in the closet, and everyone who knew her had only good things to say. Her boyfriend was cleared as well as coworkers, friends, and family. She wasn't raped, and she had a small change purse in her pocket with $75 still in it. It was a senseless murder with no motive known to date." Sheriff Gardner, a robust middle-aged man, scratched his head. Pulling his chair closer to his desk, he rested his chin on a fist, eyes jetting back and forth between Kelly and Joe.

"How long are you going to be in Sedona?" he asked Joe.

"Leaving tomorrow. Why?"

"Not sure yet—just wondering. I'll wait and see what comes back from ABI on the lab results." He then addressed Kelly. "If you're available tomorrow, I'd like you to meet me at Bell Rock in the morning so you can show me exactly where you found the knife. Would that be a problem?"

"No, not at all. Since I'm not working at the moment, my schedule is pretty flexible." Less tense than when she first arrived, Kelly asked, "What time did you have in mind?"

"I should be over there by nine a.m."

"Okay, I'll be sure to be there."

"Are we through here?" asked Joe.

Sheriff Gardner reached in his desk and took out a pad. "Before you leave, write down your names, addresses, and phone numbers should I need to get in touch with either of you." Kelly took the pad first and entered her information, then gave it to Joe.

Extending her hand, Kelly said, "Well, Sheriff, I guess I'll see you in the morning."

When Joe finished writing down his information, he laid the pad on the sheriff's desk and shook his hand.

"I appreciate the two of you bringing the knife here. If you don't mind, Ms. Murphy, I'd like to keep the backpack until we know what, if anything, we're dealing with."

"As far as I'm concerned, you can have it. I doubt I'll be using it again anyway."

Chapter Fifteen

While drinking her morning coffee, Kelly thought back over the events of the day before and wondered why finding that bloody knife had distorted her thinking. Her concerns of being questioned by the sheriff now seemed irrational, at best. *Normally, I'm a very level-headed, disciplined person with good judgment,* she told herself. *I must need more coffee.* As she passed by the fireplace she paused to look at the picture on the mantle above. It was of two friends, Kelly and Tara, hiking on the Colorado National Monument.

Tara, I guess the anniversary of your death has affected me more than I realized. This past year seems like a blur, and I certainly haven't been myself. I've made a lot of changes without understanding why. Hopefully, now that I'm in Sedona, things will start to make sense. Taking a sip of coffee, she glanced at the clock. *Well, if I'm to meet Sheriff Gardner by nine o'clock, I'd better get moving.*

When she drove into the parking lot, she noticed the sheriff's vehicle and pulled up beside it. Sheriff Gardner got out of the SUV and came over to open her door.

"Good morning, Ms. Murphy."

"And a good morning to you, Sheriff." Stepping out of the car, Kelly noticed the sheriff holding a piece of paper. "Is that a map of the hiking trails?"

"Actually, it covers the whole Bell Rock area. There are more trees around here than I remembered. It's possible we could have overlooked one when we were searching for the murder weapon, but we assumed the murderer might get rid of the knife here, and we were pretty thorough in our search." He motioned for Kelly to go ahead. "Ms. Murphy, I'll follow you." Kelly started up the main trail and then veered to her right, almost making a U-turn. There were more trees along this path. As they progressed further, they encountered low-wire fencing—some smooth and some barbed—running along the sides of the trail. When she came to an open area where the wire was smooth and lower, Kelly stepped over it and went straight toward the familiar juniper. As she got closer—remembering that frightening ordeal—her heart began to race. Comforted by the sheriff's presence, she took a deep breath and tried to relax.

"Is this where you normally hike when you're at Bell Rock?" asked the sheriff.

"No, I usually stay on the trail that we were on first, which leads up to the rock formations and ledges around Bell Rock. I have a special place up there where I like to sit and meditate. When I'm through meditating, I decide if I have time to wander and go off in different directions before calling it a day." When she got to the juniper tree, she stopped and knelt down on the hard surface and pointed to the spot where she had dug up the knife. "This is where I found it."

Sheriff Gardner stared at the tree, then stooped to take a closer look at the place where the knife was discovered. After studying the ground beneath the juniper, he stood to get a better look of the area around him. "What made you climb over the wire and come to this particular tree?"

"Instinct, I guess," Kelly replied, not knowing what else to say.

"I'd say that's some damn good instinct!"

"I know it sounds strange, but every time I came this way, I was drawn to this tree." Patting the side of the trunk as she stood up, she added, "I find the aging, gnarled old juniper to be stunningly beautiful! I don't know. Maybe I was meant to find the weapon."

The sheriff shook his head. "I'd be having my doubts about you if I hadn't already had you checked out."

"What do you mean?"

"I called that newspaper you said you worked for."

"*Used* to work for," she corrected.

"They put me on with someone named Stan."

"You spoke with Stan?"

"Yeah. He told me you were a little out there."

"What!?"

"Well, not exactly in those words. I think what he said was 'she has a keen sense of judgment and a sixth sense like no one I've ever worked with.' That's probably more accurate. I just condensed it a little."

Kelly smiled. She was pleased to see that the sheriff had a sense of humor, and it felt good to hear—even if indirectly—from Stan.

The sheriff was quick to get back to the task at hand. "How far from here was the stranger when you saw him coming toward you?"

Kelly walked off an estimate of where she thought she first saw him when he began his approach. The sheriff made a note.

"This *is* a big old tree. I can't imagine it wasn't looked at when we conducted our search."

"Maybe whoever murdered Melanie Davies buried the knife after you were through searching the area."

"That doesn't make sense. Why risk it? You'd think he'd want to clean off any incriminating evidence, and then get rid of it—unless he had to dispose of it quickly."

"Maybe he has a family and didn't want to chance taking it back to his place. Or, if he's a serial killer, he could have buried the knife after the area was searched with the intent of digging it up one day and keeping it as his trophy."

"I've known of such cases," said Sheriff Gardner, "although I haven't heard of a serial killer on the loose in the state of Arizona. But I appreciate your thoughts, Ms. Murphy. I'll do some checking when I get back to the office. In the meantime, thank you for your help. If I have any more questions, I'll give you a call. I'm going to stick around and check the area further, but you're free to go. I don't need to keep you any longer."

Before leaving, Kelly took one last lingering look at the gnarly old juniper. She felt a sense of accomplishment. She'd promised to call Joe when she got back to the condo and let him know how the morning went, and then the plan was for him to come over. The neighborhood potluck was that afternoon, and since Joe was on a later flight, she'd managed to talk him into going with her. He told her he wasn't thrilled about attending a potluck with people he didn't know, but it beat the alternative of having to sit in an airport for hours.

Chapter Sixteen

"**I** don't know how you talked me into this," Joe grunted.

"I'm not excited about going either, but I promised Gina. At least it's a luncheon potluck, so you'll have plenty of time to get to Flagstaff and make your flight."

"I'd rather spend the time at your place drinking coffee and discussing the Melanie Davies case." He refrained from saying that he wasn't sure when he'd see her again, and he would have enjoyed some quality time with her—without the distraction of people he didn't know.

"Oh, there's Gina. Come on, I'll introduce you to her." Gina was with several other people who were gathered at a long table that appeared to have been set up to accommodate all the food.

"Kelly! I'm so glad you could make it!"

"I only brought deviled eggs. I hope that's okay."

"That's perfect! I think you're the only one who brought deviled eggs, and they seem to go well with everything." Gina looked up at Joe. "And who's the handsome stranger with you?"

"I seem to have been replaced with eggs," Joe teased.

"Only momentarily," blushed Kelly. "Gina, this is an old friend, Joe Conrad. His flight doesn't leave until later tonight so I invited him to come along with me. I hope that's okay."

"Of course it is. Hi, Joe. Very nice to meet you. I'm Gina Sanders, Kelly's *new* friend." Someone with an armful of food called to Gina from across the parking lot. "I think I'm being paged and it looks like they could use some help. That's Carl and Mary Wilkins, and they've lived here for two years. Kelly, I'll catch up with you guys in a little bit. Why don't you set the eggs down and mingle a while? Everyone should be here shortly." Carl called out to Gina again. "Coming," she assured him, taking off in their direction.

"She's quite a knockout! Look at those long legs and beautiful blond hair ... and that body!" Joe said, hoping to get a rise out of Kelly.

"Yes, she *is* quite attractive," replied Kelly nonchalantly, "and she's a very nice person, too," she added, placing the eggs next to a pan of baked beans.

"So, *she's* the clairvoyant. I wonder if she read my mind."

"I doubt it. She can only read a mind if you have one," Kelly chided back.

Joe laughed. "Come on, let's meet some of your neighbors."

They walked around, introducing themselves and chatting with those who seemed to be the most outgoing. When Gina announced that it was time to eat, the lines began to form. Kelly and Joe seated themselves at one of the makeshift tables and waited until last to grab their plates and get in line. Gina came over and asked Kelly if she'd save a seat for her.

"I have to return a quick call, but I'll be right back, and I'd love to sit with you both."

"We'd love to have you join us," said Kelly.

"Psychic, huh?" Joe murmured as Gina walked away.

"She's also a great artist! That reminds me, I was so preoccupied yesterday with telling you about finding the knife and the article on Melanie Davies—not to mention going to the sheriff's office—that I forgot to show you the painting Gina gave me as a welcoming gift. It's a beautiful rendition of Bell Rock. She captured several of the hiking trails, and if you look closely, you can even see a tree that resembles the one where I found the knife."

"Really? I'd like to see it."

"When we leave here, if you have time to come in for a minute, I'll show you the painting. Maybe you could even help me find a place to hang it."

"I'd like that."

By the time Gina returned, Joe and Kelly were already halfway through their meal. "Thanks for saving room for me. I had no intention of being gone that long."

Through the rest of the meal, Gina kept a running conversation with the neighbors who were seated at their table and always included Kelly in the discussions. Joe politely asked a few questions, but he mostly just listened.

"So, Kelly, are you liking it here in God's Country?" Asked the pudgy, rosy-cheeked, white-haired gentleman sitting across from her.

"Kelly, Walter's our go-to guy if you have any questions about Sedona or the surrounding area. He's lived here most of his life and is very knowledgeable."

"That's good to know," said Kelly. "I'll keep that in mind. And, yes, Walter, I'm enjoying Sedona very much."

When the group began dispersing, Kelly offered to help with any remaining cleanup. Gina thanked her and said it wasn't necessary since those who brought a table or tablecloth were already getting everything ready to go. "That's the nice part about potlucks: Everyone takes their stuff home with them. Kelly, let's try to get together for lunch next week. I have some time Thursday or Friday if you do."

"I'm sure that I do, and I would like that, Gina."

"It was very nice meeting you, Joe. Maybe I'll see you again sometime."

"Same here, Gina."

Gina walked briefly with them as they headed back to Kelly's condo. She pointed to a building and told Kelly that her unit was number 204 on the second floor. Their complexes were across the street from each other, but it wasn't too far of a walk. "Kelly, I forgot to ask you—do you know that man standing over there by the dumpster?"

After looking in his direction, Kelly shook her head. "I don't think so. I doubt I'd know him, I haven't met very many people here. Why? Is he a neighbor?"

"I'm not sure. I don't remember him from delivering the invitations. But this is the third time I've seen him here today, and each time he seems to be looking in your direction. I just wondered if you might have met him somewhere and mentioned that you were going to be here. Maybe you just look familiar to him."

"He's probably one of Kelly's secret admirers and he's intimidated by my presence. He's waiting for me to leave so he can come over and talk to her," Joe teased. "But on second thought, it seems strange that he'd just be standing there."

Trying not to appear obvious, Kelly glanced his way again. She found herself thinking about the stranger at Bell Rock. Aware that he was being watched, the man casually turned and slowly walked away as if not to raise curiosity.

"If he's a neighbor, he's either very standoffish or shy. Too bad he didn't join us—he doesn't know what he missed," said Gina.

Kelly watched the stranger leave. "Gina, do you have a neighbor whose wife just had back surgery?" She didn't want to alarm her by telling her what happened at Bell Rock, but she thought it was a good opportunity to play detective.

"Not that I know of. Why do you ask?"

"I met someone from out of town when I was hiking. He said he was here on a visit to help his cousin take care of the kids while his wife recovered from back surgery. I just thought maybe that guy was the same person."

"Anything's possible. I'm sure I haven't met all my neighbors, but I don't remember seeing any children over here, and I haven't heard of anyone that's recently had back surgery."

Joe shot Kelly a look of concern. She shook her head to reassure him that she didn't believe it was the same man she'd met at Bell Rock. They said good-bye to Gina and headed back to Kelly's condo. Once out of Gina's view, Joe paused. "Kelly, if you think there's any similarity, or any chance at all that this guy could be the same man that was at Bell Rock, I'll go look for him."

"If you go after this guy, will you go after the next, and the next, and so on just because I'm going to question every new face I see? I can't let this cripple me. I'm a strong person, and I'll use good judgment. I'll go on the offense and I'll help the sheriff in any way I can. Besides, we don't even know yet if the knife is the murder weapon. If the man at Bell Rock was telling the truth, and he's really only here for a visit, he wouldn't have known Melanie. I don't know why he acted the way he did, or what his motives were, but I can't let him paralyze me with fear. Joe, I won't be a victim."

Chapter Seventeen

Admiring the painting of Bell Rock—which now, thanks to Joe, was hanging above the mantle, replacing the picture of a flower garden—Kelly clutched her cup of coffee, and wondered how long it would be before she'd see Joe again. *It's been a strange couple of days, and through it all I've come to realize how much I miss having him in my life. I don't know if that's good or bad, but as long as I can keep things in perspective, it shouldn't be a problem. Neither of us needs a long-distance relationship, but there's nothing wrong with being friends and staying in touch with each other.*

Finding the knife and getting Joe and the sheriff involved, and discussing the Davies case with Joe had helped Kelly make a decision. Setting the coffee down, she picked up her cell and called Dan Mathews.

"Hi, Dan. This is Kelly Murphy. I'm very interested in the position you offered ... that is, if it's still available. When it's convenient, I'd like to talk with you further," she blurted without hesitation.

"Kelly! Great to hear from you! I was hoping you'd call. Yes, the position is still open and I'd love for you to fill it. Can you come in tomorrow? I'd like to show you around, introduce you to everyone, and go over your job description—which I've given a lot of thought to."

"I'd like that. I'd also like to talk to you about a case that you might have some knowledge of."

"Are you referring to the homicide of Melanie Davies?"

"Yes, how did you know?"

"Talked to Joe this morning. He called to see if I knew anything about it. He also told me about the creep who came at you."

"Yeah, that was pretty intense. I should have known Joe would call you. Before he left last night, he mentioned there might be a possibility you'd know something. So do you?"

"I know *of* the case, but not the ins and outs of it. You and Joe probably know more than I do. I was contacted by Melanie's parents several weeks ago. Frustrated with the lack of information they were receiving from the sheriff's office, they decided to hire a private investigator. I was referred to them, but with Tom leaving and one of my PIs in the hospital recovering from knee surgery, I couldn't take on any more clients at that time."

"Interesting. Do you know if Mr. and Mrs. Davies hired anyone else?"

"Not sure. I hadn't given anymore thought to it until Joe called this morning. I do remember giving them a couple of names of other investigators that I've worked with in the past, but I don't know if they ever called them.

"Kelly, Joe told me about the knife and how you found it. He also told me about the two of you meeting with Sheriff Gardner, so I can appreciate your interest in the case. I don't know if the sheriff would tell you anything relating to his findings from ABI, but since you spent a little time with him at Bell Rock, it wouldn't hurt to call and just see what he has to say. We can talk about it when you come in tomorrow and discuss at that time whether the firm wants to get involved. If so, then I'll call the Davies to see how they're progressing and if they need our help."

Kelly thanked Dan and told him she'd be in his office by nine a.m. She no sooner hung up when the doorbell rang.

"Good morning, Gina."

"Hi, Kelly. You got a minute?"

"Sure, come on in. I have some coffee left. Would you like a cup?"

"No, thanks. I already had my fill." Gina noticed the painting. "Wow! That's a great place to have Bell Rock. I knew this is where it belonged."

"Gina, come over here," Kelly said as she moved in front of the painting. "Stand directly in front of it and look out the sliding doors." Gina did as instructed. She could see what Kelly was getting at: The top half of the painting was almost a carbon copy of the view from outside Kelly's balcony. "When I look at it, I feel like I'm bringing Bell Rock inside my condo. The only thing I can't see from my balcony at this distance are the multitude of trees and trails that you were able to capture in the painting. I'm so impressed with your work, Gina. I think you should pursue more of your artistic side." She wanted to add, and quit wasting your time on psychic readings, but she didn't.

Kelly looked at her watch and wondered why Gina wasn't on her way to the Center by now. "Are you off today?' she asked.

"I purposely didn't schedule any readings until late afternoon. I have some errands to run this morning—bank, post office, and shopping for a new outfit. I have a friend in Phoenix who's getting married next weekend. That's one reason I stopped by."

"Oh?"

"The wedding isn't until Sunday afternoon, but I'm going down on Friday for Sandy's bachelorette party. I'll come home late on Sunday after the reception. I wanted to let you know in case you stopped by or tried to call, because I'll probably have my phone off most of the weekend. I also stopped by to see if you'd like to meet me for lunch today—that is, if you don't already have plans," she said as she intentionally looked around the condo toward the bedroom.

Kelly smiled. She knew what Gina was hinting at. "Joe isn't here. He left last night. But if he were here, he'd be quite visible and not hiding in a room he's never seen before. I told you, we're just friends."

Gina laughed. "Well, he seems very nice. I'd like to know more about him so, are you free for lunch?"

"Yes. Just name the time and place and I'll meet you there."

Chapter Eighteen

She arrived at the restaurant a few minutes early. Kelly and Gina agreed to meet at Javelina's, a southwestern restaurant located at the end of a strip mall. An Irish pub sat on the other end of the mall, with several unique gift shops in between. Since Kelly was early, she decided to browse through one of the shops. As she meandered around the display of pottery, quartz, and crystal, a large colorful glass plate positioned on a stand in the window caught her eye. Making her way toward the plate, she could see her parked car through the window and noticed a man peering in on the passenger side. Assuming that he'd parked next to her, she expected him to be on his way, but he seemed to linger. There was just enough distance from Kelly's car and the store window to prevent her from getting a clear view of the man, but she did notice that he appeared to be of average height and slightly chubby. Forgetting about the glass plate, she made her way to the door, but by the time she stepped out, the man was walking away. She shrugged it off as a curious bystander and headed for the restaurant.

Gina was already seated in a booth and waved Kelly over. "I got here a few minutes early. Is a booth okay, or would you rather have a table?"

"No, I like a booth. This is perfect."

After they placed their order, Gina began to quiz Kelly on how her visit went with Joe. At first Kelly felt awkward. She'd never talked about her personal life with anyone except Tara, but she liked Gina and found her easy to talk to. Before she knew it, she was telling her all about Joe and how they met during a snowstorm in Cripple Creek. She even told Gina about Tara and how Joe worked with her to help solve Tara's murder. She spoke freely of the past but stopped short of mentioning the knife she found at Bell Rock, the encounter with the stranger, and the death of Melanie Davies.

Gina shook her head. "You've had a tough year, Kelly. I'm beginning to understand your relationship with Joe, and I can appreciate a little more why you left your job and moved away. Maybe, subconsciously, you felt you needed a change of scenery to move forward and shed that phase of your life. Grief can cause a person to become immobile and unable to function, at times, hovering in a state of inertia. Compound that with Tara's murderer coming after you, and you're also dealing with the loss of feeling safe and secure, as well as losing your ability to trust." Gina paused when she saw the waitress coming with their food.

"I have a chicken fajita salad for you," she said placing the bowl in front of Gina, "and a chicken sandwich for you," she added, setting the plate down for Kelly. "I'll check back in a few minutes. Do you want anything to drink besides water?" Both women indicated that water was enough, and the waitress went on her way.

Gina took a bite of her salad and then continued. "I think for you, Kelly, getting away was what you needed to do. You may not know why now, but I have a sense it will become clear sooner than not." Taking another bite of salad, she said, "Have you thought about working somewhere in the area?"

"Funny you should ask. I just accepted a position this morning with an investigative agency based in Flagstaff. I'm to start tomorrow." Kelly went on to tell Gina about Dan Mathew's phone call and his connection to Joe. "I'm still not clear on what exactly I'll be doing, but I guess I'll find out soon enough." She noticed Gina smiling. "What's the smile for?" she asked.

"I'm glad you accepted the job. I have a good feeling about it, and I think your apprehension will leave as soon as you walk into his office. It's a good thing, Kelly. Trust yourself, your ability, and your judgment, and soon you'll realize that it's where you're supposed to be."

"Is this the friend talking or the psychic?"

"Maybe a little of both," Gina said, grinning as she took another bite of food.

Kelly left it at that and finished eating her sandwich. Changing subjects, she talked more with Gina about her friend's wedding.

Gina glanced at her watch. "I wish I had more time, but I guess I'd better go—don't want to leave my client waiting. I've enjoyed talking with you and learning more about you. Kelly, I hope we can do it again real soon."

"I'd like that, but next time it's your turn to do most of the talking."

Their cars were parked near each other, so they walked out together and through the parking lot. Gina paused and turned to Kelly, "I'm not trying to read you, but I have a gut feeling that there's something weighing heavy on your mind. Would you like to come over tonight and talk about it?"

Kelly thought about her hike on Bell Rock and everything that took place when she found that knife. She already trusted Gina, and she knew that she could talk to her, but she wasn't ready. "There's nothing to talk about, but thanks for the offer."

Gina raised an eyebrow. "Okay, but if you ever want to talk, the offer stands."

"I know. Thank you."

Chapter Nineteen

Before meeting with Dan the next morning, Kelly wanted to get in touch with Sheriff Gardner. She tried calling him before her lunch with Gina but he didn't answer. It was afternoon now and she hoped he'd be in his office.

"Sheriff Gardner here."

"Hi, Sheriff. This is Kelly Murphy ..." Before she could say anything else, he interrupted.

"Ah, yes, Ms. Murphy. Just the person I want to talk to."

Kelly was surprised by his comment. "Does this have anything to do with the location of where I found the knife?" she asked, feeling a little hesitant.

"No, No. I'm clear on that. I just got the report back from ABI. No fingerprints were found, but they did find DNA, other than that of Melanie Davies. Kelly—you did say I could call you Kelly?"

"Of course," she said, wondering why he was voluntarily giving information about the case without her asking.

"Kelly, the sheriff's office here is small. There's just me and Deputy Brian Welks. Our resources are limited.

After talking with your former editor, Stan, I have a better understanding of your background. The other day when you and Joe Conrad were here in my office, Mr. Conrad mentioned that you were interviewing with an investigative firm out of Flagstaff." He paused before continuing. "It might be better to continue this discussion in person. Are you available to stop by here in the morning?"

"No, I'm sorry, but I'm not available. I've decided to take the position that I interviewed for with Dan Mathews, and I'm to meet with him in the morning. I'm not sure of my hours, but considering the distance, I'm hoping I can work some of the time from my condo. That's something I have to talk to Dan about when I meet with him."

"Okay, then would you give me a call when you're leaving Flagstaff? I'll plan to be here if it's not too late. Maybe you could stop by on your way home."

Curious, Kelly thought it might be better to meet with Sheriff Gardner before seeing Dan. "I could come by now, if you have the time," she suggested.

"That works. I'll see you in a little bit."

Walking into the sheriff's office, Kelly saw him sitting behind his desk sifting through a stack of paperwork. He looked up when he saw her come in.

"You see all this, Ms. Murphy ... ?"

"Kelly," she interrupted

"Yeah, don't mind me. There will be times I call you Kelly, and other times I'll call you Ms. Murphy. That's just how I am, so bear with me."

"Sure. Sorry to interrupt you."

Staring at the stack on his desk, he said, "This is what I've collected in the last few months on the Melanie Davies case." He lifted up a small file, "This is the coroner's report." Pointing to the mass of files that remained he added, "Most of these files contain the interviews we've done on anyone and everyone who knew Melanie Davies."

Fixated on the files, Kelly said, "I gather this has something to do with what you wanted to talk to me about."

"As a matter-of-fact, it does. I've gone through these files several times, and I'm wondering if I'm missing something. Nothing stands out as unusual or suspicious in any of the interviews—at least that I can tell. All have alibis, and anyone that I might have had questions about ... well, it seems their statements at the time of Ms. Davies' death, checks out." He shook his head. "Never thought I'd be saying this, Kelly—especially since I hate when PIs interfere with my job—but I could use a second pair of eyes on this case, and you *are* the one who found the knife."

"First, Sheriff Gardner, I'm not a private investigator."

"Yeah, yeah, I know that, but you might soon be working for one. By the way, you can drop the 'Sheriff Gardner.' Just call me Matt."

Kelly smiled. "Okay. By the way, Matt, have you had time to check with the police department to see if they've had any reports of women being followed or frightened by a strange man?"

"I did check, and they didn't have any complaints of that nature. Kelly, I was hoping you might have some time this week to come in and go through some of these files. I'd like to know if anything stands out to you that might suggest taking a second look. I realize it's a lot to ask, and I'm not sure how you'll be compensated since we work on a tight budget here, but if you're interested, I'll figure out something."

Kelly felt the adrenaline flow and her heart begin to pound. She didn't know why—maybe it was because she was drawn to that old tree and then found the knife—but she felt connected to Melanie Davies. She wondered if she could persuade Dan to get involved. *If Melanie's family hired him to help solve the case, then the sheriff wouldn't have to worry about the monetary aspect of it.*

"Matt, I would like to help, and there might be a way to do so without upsetting the budget. Let me get back to you after my meeting with Dan Mathews tomorrow." Before she turned to leave, Kelly thought of something else that she wanted to ask the sheriff. "You said that ABI found DNA on the knife, but I take it there wasn't a match in the database."

"No. The guy dosen't show up on radar. Either this is the first time he's ever done anything like this, or he's careful not to get caught—which makes him even more dangerous."

Chapter Twenty

After meeting with Sheriff Gardner, Kelly drove through the parking lot around Bell Rock. The heat of the day hadn't subsided yet, and there were only a couple of parked cars. She wondered if one of them had been there the other day and wished she'd been more aware of the vehicles parked there at that time. This evening, everything felt normal, and she didn't feel uneasy, but she didn't have a desire to stay and visit her favorite old juniper tree either. She hadn't planned on talking to Gina about all this, but on her way home she found herself on Gina's doorstep, ringing the bell.

"Kelly, what a nice surprise. Come on in," Gina said, holding the door for her.

"Hi, Gina. I didn't expect to be stopping by tonight, but here I am."

"I'm glad you did. I just made a pot of coffee. Would you like a cup?"

"I would, thanks. I hope I'm not interrupting your dinner."

"Not at all. I usually eat a big lunch and then nibble at night. Have a seat," she said, pointing to a tan leather sofa. "I'll get our coffee. Do you take sugar or cream?"

"Just black, thank you." Kelly couldn't help but notice all the paintings of the Sedona area hanging on the small living room wall. "Gina, did you paint all these?"

"As a matter-of-fact, I did." She set two cups of coffee down on a small hand-sculpted coffee table. Gina's condo was smaller than Kelly's, but everything in it was top quality. "There's so much beauty around Sedona that's it's easy to get caught up in it," said Gina.

Looking at three paintings above the sofa behind her, Kelly pointed to the one in the center. "Is that Cathedral Rock?"

"Yes. Actually, all three of them are—just different views. I have too many paintings in here, but I don't know where else to put them. You should see my bedroom! That's where I paint, and I have two on easels right now. I don't paint every day, but I leave my stuff out rather than having to put it up every time I'm through. If it wasn't such a mess in there I'd show you, but I'll save that for another time, because I don't think that's why you came over anyway."

Kelly took a deep breath and picked up her coffee. She held it tightly, as if needing the support, and sipped it slowly before saying anything. "As I mentioned, I wasn't planning to stop by—but for some reason—I did."

"Maybe you just need someone to talk to other than Joe. No disrespect intended, but sometimes women just need to talk to other women."

Kelly smiled, "Or at least someone close by." Kelly began to bring Gina up to date on everything that had transpired during the past week including her visit with Sheriff Gardner, but she chose to minimize her encounter with the stranger. She said that he may have been curious to see what she'd found and stopped short of describing the fear she felt.

"Wow! Welcome to Sedona," said Gina. "No wonder I sensed you had a lot going on. Now I know why I felt your working with Dan would be a good thing. If Dan will get involved in the Davies case—and I think he will—I know that you will be a tremendous asset to him, the Davies family, and the sheriff. Of course, you'll approach it from your curious reporter's viewpoint, but your intuitive side is going to kick into high gear, and your instinct will dominate your direction."

Kelly bristled. "Reporter's—and even women's—instinct I can accept, but please stop referring to my sense of good judgment as my 'intuitive side.' I'd like to think that having had a good mentor, and my experience at the newspaper is what directs me."

"I do seem to hit a sensitive spot with you, don't I?" Gina said. "Call it a gut feeling, or whatever you want, all I'm saying is, just trust yourself. You're not always going to have evidence or proof before you, but when you sense something strongly, go with it. I'm not sure you're telling me everything about the man you met, but if you had a concern or negative vibe about him, don't dismiss it."

Kelly was quiet for a moment, as if reflecting on Gina's words, and then she took another swallow of her coffee. "Gina, I know I sense things at times, but if I were really intuitive—as you suggest—then wouldn't I have known that Tara was in danger?"

"Not necessarily. I don't know why this is, and it's not always the case, but sometimes it's harder to sense danger or trouble with those closest to us—including ourselves. Like I said, it's not always that way, but I know at times it is for me, especially when it comes to reading myself. When Tara died, you were busy and preoccupied, but after the fact, your senses did escalate. You knew deep down that her death wasn't an accident.

"Intuition is not the same for everyone. There will be times when you have feelings that are unfamiliar, so you'll tend to ignore them. All I'm asking is that you try to be more receptive to those feelings. I think on some level you know what I'm talking about, and I think that's why you came over. You need someone to talk to when you're feeling something that other people may not understand. Kelly, we connected from the first moment we met, and I know you feel as comfortable with me as I do with you. I also know you realize there's some merit in what I'm saying."

"I do trust you, Gina, and I must appreciate your insight, because otherwise I don't believe I would have told you all that I have. I wish I understood why the unsolved murder of Melanie has grabbed me the way that it has. There has to be more to it than my finding the knife. The whole thing seems strange, especially the way I felt drawn to that old juniper tree."

"Almost as if Melanie's reaching out to you," Gina said.

Kelly was quick to respond. "Well, I wouldn't go that far."

"Okay, maybe not—but *maybe*. For some reason you've been drawn into this, and now even the sheriff wants your help. It's obvious that you're going to be involved, and that may become clearer when you meet with Dan in the morning."

"I'm not sure that he'll be interested."

"Things will be different in the morning, you'll see."

Chapter Twenty-One

Returning from Gina's, Kelly noticed her cell on the coffee table and realized that she'd forgotten to take it with her when she went to meet the sheriff. There was a message from Joe. He said he was just checking to see how things were going and he'd call again tomorrow, or she could call him when she had a minute. Kelly considered returning his call because she wanted to tell him about her meeting with Matt, but she decided to wait until after she met with Dan.

The next morning, when Kelly arrived at Dan's office, he wasted no time in showing her around. Taking her by the arm, he guided her through the complex and introduced her to the rest of his staff, saving Jennifer Roberts for last. Unlike the cubicles that most of the staff worked out of, Jennifer's office was similar to Dan's, and had glass walls, so they could see that she was on the phone. While they waited, Dan took the opportunity to fill Kelly in on Jennifer's background.

"Jennifer came aboard fifteen years ago. She started as a secretary, but it wasn't long before I learned how interested and fascinated she was in criminal law. I like studying people, and I soon realized what a gem I had in

Jennifer. I suggested we have a cup of coffee so I could learn more about her. She told me she'd been a paralegal a few years before, but had taken time off when she became pregnant with twins. After they were born, she decided to be a stay-at-home mom until the boys started school. Feeling rusty from not working for a few years, and not wanting to work overtime as she had before, she answered our ad for a secretary position. I wasn't involved in hiring her! Jack saw to that. She's amazing on the computer, very fast and rarely makes a mistake. Anyway, after having coffee with her on that day fifteen years ago, I encouraged her to get her private investigator's license and promised that any overtime would be at her discretion. The rest is history. Some of the time Jen—she likes to be called that—and Jack work as a team, similar to how Tom and I worked. I tell you all this because Jen will be a good person to go to if I'm not available or if you need to consult with someone. She's easy to get along with and very willing to help."

"Go to for what?" Kelly asked, still questioning exactly what Dan had in mind for her.

He smiled. "I have a lot to discuss with you, Kelly, most of which I think you'll appreciate. For now, let's go in and meet Jen." He opened the door just as she was walking toward them.

"You must be Kelly," she said extending her hand. "It's so nice to meet you."

Jen was warm and friendly, and immediately Kelly felt at ease. "Dan's been telling me all about you," she said.

"I hope not everything," Jen teased. "Come and sit down and give me a chance to debunk the lies Dan's been telling you." She winked. "I have a few tales of my own." Dan threw up his hands in jest, as if surrendering to something he'd prefer not be told.

Kelly thought Jen looked young to have twins who would now be about twenty. She was a couple of inches shorter than Kelly's five-foot-six frame and appeared to have perfect posture. Her short brown hair, in a pixie style, was combed forward and surrounded her heart-shaped face. She was cute with a petite figure, and her deep blue eyes sparkled.

After spending about ten minutes with Jen, Kelly and Dan went back to his office. "So, Kelly, what do you think of the place?"

"I like it. It's not as large as I first thought it was, and yet everyone seems to have plenty of space. It doesn't feel crowded. I wouldn't have guessed a dozen people work here—all of whom, by the way, are very nice."

"Everyone, from my clerical employees up to my partners, are very important to me."

"I can tell that," she said.

Dan leaned back in his chair and rubbed his forehead. "I especially wanted you to meet Jen because now that Tom's gone, we might need Jen's or Jack's help from time to time. Kelly, you asked me about Melanie Davies. Well, the strangest thing happened. After you talked to me about her—geez, it couldn't have been more than a few hours—I got a call from Melanie's mother asking if we would please reconsider looking into her daughter's murder. She and her husband had been trying to do some of their own investigating but, being novices, they hadn't accomplished very much. I don't know if the sheriff has this information, but Mrs. Davies told me she had talked to one of Melanie's friends who remembered seeing Melanie in a coffee shop with a man that the friend didn't recognize just a few days before she was murdered. The friend was passing by the shop on her way to an appointment and glanced in and saw them. She didn't think much of it at the time, assuming that it might have been one of Melanie's coworkers."

"Interesting. Does this mean you're going to take the case?" Kelly asked.

"After speaking with Mrs. Davies, and considering your interest, I talked it over with Jen and Jack. Sometimes cases like this can be all-consuming, and I wasn't sure I'd have the time. Mrs. Davies said she and her husband would spare no expense when it came to solving their daughter's murder. They want justice for Melanie. I didn't want to accept their money without knowing if we'd be able to give them the time they deserved. Jack's busy doing some background work for a colleague of ours, but Jen said she'd help out in a pinch. This is the type of case that either Jen or Jack would be able to pick up on right away if we needed their help, and that's why I wanted to talk to them first. Once I knew I'd have Jen as a backup, I called Mrs. Davies and told her we'd take the case. Kelly, I believe that once we start working together, your position will become more defined. For now, I'd like you to come aboard as my assistant. Will that work for you?"

"I'd like that." Kelly didn't need to think about it. She knew it was what she wanted to do, but there was one thing she still needed to discuss. "Dan, my only concern at this point is the commute." She talked about the possibility of working from her condo, and Dan didn't think that it would be a problem. He told her they'd probably be working out in the field more than the office anyway.

Kelly told Dan about her visit with Matt Gardner and the information he shared about the DNA found on the knife. "So apparently this person isn't in the system. They couldn't find a match. Matt also showed me a stack of files containing all the interviews the sheriff's office conducted. After checking into my background, he asked if I'd be willing to review them and see if anything unusual stands out."

Dan responded enthusiastically, "Kelly, that's great! You can start with the interviews, and I'll call and set up a time to meet with the Davies. I'll also get the name of the friend they told me about and call you with it. If you come across her interview, check to see if she mentioned anything about seeing Melanie with someone prior to her death—and if so—did she give a description."

Chapter Twenty-Two

Returning Joe's call, Kelly told him about her plans to meet with the sheriff. "Matt wants me to go over the interviews at his office. It's a pain, and I'd prefer to do it here, but I can understand why he wouldn't want me to take the files off the premises."

"If you come across anything that you'd like to explore further, maybe he'll let you make copies," said Joe. "It sounds like you have a couple of busy days, Kelly."

"Yeah, I guess I *have* rattled on, but I did spare you my luncheon with Gina and my visit with her last night."

"I take it the two of you are becoming pretty good friends."

"It seems that way to me, and it feels good. She's the only person I've really gotten to know in Sedona. I like her, and I enjoy talking with her."

"I'm glad. I'm also glad you'll be working with Dan. He's a great guy!" There was a pause before he continued. "Kelly, on a more serious note, have you given any thought to when—if ever—you'll return to Colorado?"

"It's funny you should ask that, because I asked myself the same question on the way home from Dan's. Joe, I'm being completely honest when I say this, but I really don't know at this point. Still, at the same time, I don't believe Sedona will be my permanent home. I think it's where I need to be right now and that's as far as I can project." She didn't tell him about her other thoughts on that drive home—how much she enjoyed seeing him and how much she regretted the distance between them. There was no need to. She knew that even if she moved back to Grand Junction, the distance still was too far for them to have a romantic relationship. She vowed she wouldn't allow herself to think of Joe that way.

"Well, at least you didn't close the door—to returning to Colorado, that is," he added. "Kelly, getting back to Melanie Davies, I know that ever since you found the knife, you feel a connection to the case, and so I'm glad Dan has taken it on. I'll be interested in what you find out when you go through the files. I'll also be curious to see what Dan learns from his visit with the Davies. I'd like you to keep me posted. I'm just a phone call away if you want to run anything by me. I wish I were closer because this is one case I'd like to be involved in."

"I'm glad you're back from your travels. It's nice to have a friend in the know to discuss this with."

"Have you consulted your psychic friend about the case?" Joe teased.

Kelly wasn't amused. "I'm assuming you mean Gina, since I don't consult psychics."

"Okay, I didn't mean to hit a nerve."

Joe had a way of pushing Kelly's buttons. *He can be so annoying at times, but at least it helps to keep my emotions in balance,* she thought.

"I'll try again. Have you spoken to Gina about finding the knife at Bell Rock?" Joe continued.

"As a matter-of-fact, I talked to her about it last night. I didn't expect to do that, but I did. It was good to bounce things off her. It felt right, and I like her perspective—which I won't get into with you. She'll be gone this weekend to a friend's wedding, and I'll be busy going through files. She gave me a key to her place and asked if I'd stop by and check on her plants in case she forgets to water them before she leaves."

"That reminds me," Joe said. "Have you seen anything of the man who was standing by the dumpster when we were leaving the potluck?"

Kelly didn't know why, but she immediately thought about the stranger peering in her car at the strip mall. She knew it wasn't the same person, because he was shorter, heavier, and wasn't as well dressed as the man by the dumpster. After her lunch with Gina, she never gave it a second thought until Joe asked his question.

"I've been on the go since then but, no, I haven't seen him. I'm sure there's nothing to it. He was probably just killing time and curious to see what was going on."

"Yeah, maybe. Hey, got another call coming in. Can you hold a sec?"

"You go on. I have a lot to do. I'll catch up with you in a few days."

Chapter Twenty-Three

It was late afternoon, and Kelly—seated across the room from the sheriff—was still looking through the files in his office. Matt was at his desk on the other side of the room. She had received a call from Dan, giving her the name of the friend who saw Melanie in the cafe just days before she died. A few minutes went by, and then Matt came over to check in with her.

"Have you come across anything that looks suspicious?" he asked. She put the file she'd been going through down on the desk and looked up at him.

"Not yet. Dan just gave me the name of the friend who raised questions with Mrs. Davies about the person she saw Melanie with in the cafe. I hadn't come across her file prior to Dan's call, but I'll search for it now." Looking at his watch, and feeling more comfortable with the idea of Kelly having the files in her possession, Matt suggested that she take them home and start fresh in the morning.

"Thank you. I could use a break, and a fresh cup of coffee in the comfort of my own home."

"You've been at it for hours. Did you even take time for lunch while I was gone?" the sheriff asked.

"No, but I've been known to skip lunch when I'm busy working on something."

"I don't want to be the cause of you losing weight. You don't look like you need to."

She smiled, "I make up for it with dinner."

"Well, you go home and have a good dinner. Take whatever files you want with you, then put them up for the night. Start again in the morning with fresh eyes."

Kelly leaned back in the chair and stretched her shoulders. "I guess I have been here longer than I realized. If you don't mind, I'd like to take most of the files with me, even some that I've already been through. I want to review them again after I've gone through the others."

"No problem. I'll give you a call tomorrow and see how it's going."

On the way home, Kelly drove by Gina's condo. Gina left early that morning for her friend's wedding, but even if she had forgotten to water her plants, Kelly felt they'd be okay until the next day. She'd go over in the morning before starting on the files. All the blinds were pulled, and Kelly wondered about the wisdom of making it so obvious that no one was at home. *But who'd be coming by,* she thought. Kelly was sure that Gina had let her neighbor's know she'd be gone for a few days.

When she got home and changed into a T-shirt and shorts, she made a sandwich and a full pot of coffee, knowing she was in for a long night. Matt's advice had fallen on deaf ears as there was no way Kelly was going to wait until morning to start on the files. One interview in particular—that of Sally Gibson, the name Dan had given her—was at the top of her list.

After sifting through a dozen or more files, she finally came to Sally's. The usual questions were asked: How do you know the deceased? Where did you meet? How long did you know her? Did she have any enemies that you're aware of? Etc., etc., etc. All looked normal until Kelly noticed that Sally's answer to one question didn't match what she'd told the Davies. "In the days before her death, did you see Melanie talking to, or mentioning having a conversation with, someone unfamiliar to her?" asked Deputy Welks. "Not that I remember," was Sally's reply. Kelly read it over and over again, making sure she hadn't missed anything. *Why didn't Sally tell him she saw Melanie in a coffee shop just days before her death with a man she didn't know? Why did she tell the Davies that, but not Brian Welks?* "Not that I remember," Kelly repeated out loud. *Surely a close friend wouldn't forget something as important as that.* She copied Sally's phone number, and then looked at her watch. *It's too late to call now, but Sally, you can be sure you'll hear from me first thing in the morning.*

The files were categorized by groups–family, friends, co-workers, acquaintances, church, clubs, and others— which consisted of people who may have done work or a service at Melanie's home, such as deliverymen, the mailman, or a newspaper carrier. The file marked "friends" was thicker than Kelly expected. Thinking of her own life, she couldn't imagine having a file consisting of friends this thick. She allowed few people to get close to her, and she'd had only one best friend—Tara. Melanie even had childhood friends who she remained close to, and they also had been interviewed. Kelly looked at her watch again. It may have been too late to call Sally, but she knew Joe would still be up.

"I agree," said Joe. "It doesn't seem like something you'd forget, friend or not, especially when asked directly. If Sally was interviewed right after Melanie's death, then that might explain it. Maybe she was too distraught to think straight at the time."

"Or she's hiding something," Kelly said.

"But then why would she tell the Davies?"

"I don't know, but I intend to find out. I'm going to call in the morning and try to meet with her."

"You might want to leave the sheriff out of the conversation—at least for now—and just say you're helping the Davies," Joe suggested.

"Good point. I'll start by trying to see her, and then see how that progresses."

Chapter Twenty-Four

Driving up to the modest ranch home, Kelly noticed it wasn't adobe or stucco style as most of the architecture in Sedona seemed to be. Still, it was painted in earth tones—more cocoa than terra cotta—and trimmed in a lighter shade of taupe. The new Toyota Prius in the driveway was a distinct contrast from the structure next to it, which appeared to have been neglected for many years. Kelly lingered a few minutes before going up to the door, mentally reviewing the list of questions she wanted to ask Sally. She wondered if her answers would explain the discrepancy in the sheriff's report.

She was greeted by a young, average-looking, petite woman who was probably in her mid-twenties. "I take it you're Kelly Murphy," she said, holding the door for her. "Come on in, we can talk in the kitchen." Kelly followed her to a small but neatly organized kitchen. At Sally's suggestion, Kelly sat down at a round oak table that was centered between the sink on one side and the refrigerator on the other. The room smelled of fresh-brewed coffee. "Would you like a cup of coffee?" Sally offered.

"I would, thank you. Just black for me." Sally brought two cups to the table and sat down across from Kelly.

"I'm not sure what Melanie's parents could have said for you to want to come out here this morning. You were a little evasive on the phone, but of course if there's anything I can do to help find out what happened to Melanie, then I certainly want to help. She didn't deserve to die. And not knowing how she died, or why, has been very frustrating. The sheriff's department hasn't released much information."

"I appreciate you taking the time to see me, Sally, especially on your day off. I'm sure that, as Melanie's friend, this has been a very difficult time for you," Kelly said warmly.

"You have no idea. I've known Melanie since grade school. We even lived in the same neighborhood for a while. I spent as much time at her house as I did my own, until I started my freshman year in high school. Her parents decided to move to a different part of town."

"That must have been tough on both of you. Do you know why they moved?"

Sally looked out the window above the sink. "Mr. Davies got a big promotion. I guess you can't blame him for wanting a better life for his family, and a safer place to live. The old neighborhood was becoming run down, and Mr. Davies suspected there was drug trafficking going on at the house at the end of our street. There were always a lot of cars coming and going. Anyway, I was concerned at first that once Melanie moved, it would have an effect on our friendship, but it never did. We saw each other at school and talked on the phone constantly, and on many occasions I even spent the night in their new home." She turned to Kelly. "That's the kind of friend and person Melanie was. No matter how many promotions—and there were many over the years that Mr. Davies got—it never changed who they were inside or where they came from. They remained humble, kind, and caring people. That's why Melanie's death doesn't make any sense. I don't know of anyone who would've wanted to harm her."

Kelly didn't want to make Sally feel uncomfortable by coming across as if she were interrogating her, but she wanted to know more about her relationship with the Davies, and why she told them, but not the sheriff about seeing Melanie with a stranger. "You're right, it doesn't make sense," responded Kelly. "I can only imagine what the Davies must be going through. Have you spoken with them lately?"

"Not for a couple of months, so I'm confused as to why you wanted to see me about something they said to you."

"Sally, I'm sorry if I gave you the impression that they spoke to me. I didn't speak directly with Mr. or Mrs. Davies. I work for someone who they hired to help solve Melanie's murder. They told him about a conversation they had with you shortly after Melanie died. We thought if you shared that conversation with us, then maybe you'd remember something else that might prove helpful."

"So you're a private investigator. I thought you were a friend of the Davies. I should have known there was more to it than that."

"Is that a problem? You *did* say you wanted to help in any way that you could. And just so you know, I'm not a private investigator, but I do work for one. The Davies hired Dan Mathews, out of Flagstaff, and I'm his assistant." Concerned that Sally would clam up, Kelly quickly continued. "After spending just these few minutes with you, I feel sure you'd want to help the Davies find Melanie's killer."

"Of course I would, but I don't see what I could have said that might be helpful."

"We're trying to trace Melanie's last few weeks before her death and who she might have had contact with, other than a coworker, friend, or family member. Mrs. Davies mentioned that you had seen Melanie having coffee in a cafe with a stranger a few days before she was found at Bell Rock. Do you remember that conversation?"

"Vaguely. It must have been when I stopped by a few weeks after the funeral. I wanted to check on them and see how they were doing. Mrs. Davies was going through a photo album. She was very emotional and asked if I could stay a while and reminisce with her. We must have gone through a dozen albums. She had a lot of pictures of different events, and several of Melanie's birthday parties with Melanie and her friends, including me," Sally smiled. "She even had an album with pictures of the two of us running through the sprinklers when we were seven or eight. I remember that we started talking about how friendly Melanie was to everyone, and how she never seemed to meet a stranger. It must've been then when I said something about seeing her in the cafe with someone that I didn't know. I probably made a comment that if he was a stranger to Melanie, he wouldn't be a stranger after spending five minutes with her. That's all there was to it. Melanie was friendly to everyone. I never gave it a second thought."

Kelly weighed the information, and while it seemed innocent enough, she thought about her own friendship with Tara. Given the circumstances of Melanie's death, she found it odd that—after the fact—Sally wouldn't have been curious about the stranger. She decided not to press the matter any further until she had a chance to talk with Mrs. Davies and get her interpretation of the conversation. If Sally was genuine, then maybe Kelly's visit would prompt her to give more thought to the day in question, and maybe she'd remember something that would prove helpful. She thanked Sally and asked her to please call if she thought of anything. Kelly didn't have a business card, but Sally wrote her phone number on a pad by the phone.

Chapter Twenty-Five

After her meeting with Sally Gibson, Kelly drove the thirty miles to Flagstaff to meet with Dan. She wanted to discuss in person any new information each might have.

"Did you believe Sally?" Dan asked.

"I'm not sure. I've no reason not to. She seemed sincere and willing to talk, but I'm having a hard time understanding her. When she was asked pointblank by the deputy if she had heard of or seen Melanie talking with anyone unfamiliar in the days before her death, Sally said no. How do you forget something like that?"

"Did you ask her?"

"No. I wanted to win her trust first, and I'd like to talk to Mrs. Davies before confronting Sally with her interview statement. It could be an innocent oversight, especially if she was used to seeing Melanie talk to people she didn't know on a regular basis. I'd like to know if the cafe was crowded, and if that was why Melanie was sharing a table with a stranger. I'd also like to know if she seemed friendly or distant toward him. To me, it seems odd that Sally didn't think much of it at the time, but Mrs. Davies thought it was important and brought it to your attention."

"Maybe Mrs. Davies is grasping at straws. She wants it to be important because she believes the sheriff's department isn't doing its job. Anyway, I have an appointment with her tomorrow at three p.m. Why don't you come with me? I'll swing by and pick you up. She's only a couple of miles from you."

"I'd like that. Now that I've spoken with Sally, I'm anxious to talk to her."

"What about Matt Gardner? When will you fill him in on your visit with Sally?"

"I'll wait until after we've had a chance to talk to Mrs. Davies. I'm not sure how much I want to share with him right now. I don't want Matt talking with Sally again just yet, at least until there's a need, if it should come to that."

Dan smiled. "Are you sure you're not a private investigator?"

"Just a good reporter who knows when to withhold information."

"I knew there was something about you I liked. We're going to make a great team, even if you don't know much about this PI stuff," he said with a wink.

On the drive back to Sedona, Kelly couldn't wipe the smile from her face. It felt good to be useful again, to have a purpose. She was five miles from home when her cell rang. It was Joe. When she answered, instead of saying hello to him, she jumped right in with everything that had transpired since they'd spoke.

"I think I got the gist of what you've said, but Kelly, could you slow down just a tad? I don't want to miss anything."

Feeling a little embarrassed, Kelly paused. "Sorry, Joe, I guess I was spewing."

"No, no, you don't need to apologize. I'm enjoying this. By the way, how does all this feel?"

Letting Joe's question sink in, she took her time before replying. "Well, I have to admit, it does feels good."

"I'm glad, Kelly. I guess this means I'm off the hook for talking to Dan about you."

"I wouldn't go that far," she said, then realized that Joe was the one who called and she hadn't given him a chance to say why. "Were you just checking in to see how things were going, or was there something specific you wanted to talk to me about?"

"A little of both. I'm trying to see when I can come to Sedona for a few days to help out. Dan has been a tremendous asset to me on a few cases, and since I have some spare time, I'd like to reciprocate."

Kelly thought it interesting that Joe said Sedona instead of Flagstaff. "If it's Dan you're wanting to work with, wouldn't it be more convenient to stay in Flagstaff?"

"Of course. Didn't I say that?"

"No, you said Sedona."

"Okay, the cat's out of the bag. Yes, I would like to help Dan, but I'd prefer to do so by staying in Sedona and help him through working with you. That is, of course, if either of you could use any extra help," Joe was quick to add.

"Since I don't pay the bills, you'd have to check with Dan. But knowing how busy the agency is right now, he'd probably like that."

"What about you, Kelly? Would you like to have someone close by—even if only for a few days—to bounce things off of?"

"Since you put it that way, how can I refuse?"

Kelly thought about all the talks she and Joe had had about what might have happened to Tara and a murder case he was working on. The more they talked, the closer they came to solving both. This time would be different, though. This time, she had feelings for Joe. She knew if she gave an inch, he'd take a mile, and emotionally she couldn't afford to do that. And she didn't want to complicate their working together.

Chapter Twenty-Six

Dan was prompt. It was exactly three o'clock when they pulled in to the Davies' driveway. The large home was surrounded by natural landscaping, featuring a variety of cactus and yucca plants that were representative of the area.

Mrs. Davies answered the door. She was not at all what Kelly had expected. Considering Melanie's age, Kelly knew Mrs. Davies could be in her late forties, but she had envisioned her to be in her fifties, slightly plump with greying hair. Instead she was slender, very attractive, and looked stylish in her white capris and navy top. Wavy shoulder-length chestnut hair—with no visible signs of grey—adorned her face.

"I've only spoken with you over the phone, so it's nice to finally meet you in person, Dan," Mrs. Davies said as she held the door for them.

"It's a pleasure meeting you, too, Mrs. Davies. I'd like to introduce you to my assistant, Kelly," he said once inside the house.

"It's nice to meet you, Kelly. I look forward to talking with both of you, and please call me Amanda."

"Thank you, Amanda," responded Kelly. "I appreciate being allowed to tag along with Dan. I know this has been a difficult time for both you and Mr. Davies."

Amanda nodded her head. "Please follow me," she said, and took them to the sunroom at the back of the house. Shaded on both sides with juniper pines, the ceiling fans were on, and it was a comfortable temperature. Four cushioned chairs were placed around a circular tiled table. Amanda had Dan and Kelly sit facing the back of the sunroom into the yard where they had beautiful views of Sedona's famous red rock formations.

"Sam will be joining us. Even though it's Saturday, he had to take a call, but he should be here shortly. He really wanted to be in on this, so I'm glad we could meet today. May I get either of you something to drink?"

"Not for me," said Dan.

"I'm fine too, but thank you," Kelly said, just as Sam Davies walked into the room.

Once the introductions were out of the way, Sam shared what little he and Amanda were able to find out on their own. "We talked to Melanie's boss and some of her coworkers, but they weren't much help. They all said she was well-liked and a conscientious worker. John, her boyfriend, was beside himself with grief. He kept repeating the same thing: 'I don't understand. I just don't get it. Who would want to hurt Melanie?' He said they had dinner out the night before she died because he was leaving town the next morning on a business trip."

"How well do you know John?" Dan asked.

"We met him about two years ago, shortly after he and Melanie started dating. I liked him right away. Last year he came to me and said that he wanted to ask her to marry him, and he hoped Amanda and I wouldn't object. He wanted our blessing before he asked Melanie. In this day and age, you don't find too many young men who would do that."

"That's for sure," echoed Amanda. "John is a wonderful man. He comes by every now and then to check on us, but I feel that *he's* the one who needs the support. We're all struggling and trying to cope, but Melanie was the love of John's life," Amanda paused then continued, "and she was our only child." She turned to Sam with tears in her eyes. He reached for her hand and squeezed it.

"We miss her so much!" he choked back the tears.

"Of course you do," Kelly said in a consoling voice. "I'm so sorry for your loss. Dan and I want to help you find out who did this to your daughter." Kelly looked to Sam and then Amanda. "I'd like to know more about Melanie. I know she liked to hike. I can relate because that's something I also enjoy.

"What kind of work did she do?"

Sam spoke up, "Melanie was a dispatcher and worked the seven a.m. to three p.m. shift. She liked to hike and take long walks at least once or twice a week. She said it relaxed her. Normally she'd go on a weekday after work if the weather was good. The weekends were kept open because that was her time with John. If John was in Sedona on the weekend, then sometimes they'd hike together, but Melanie usually went to Phoenix to be with him."

"Phoenix? So John didn't live in Sedona?" Dan interrupted.

"No," said Amanda. "He works for a large insurance company in Phoenix as an underwriter. Most of the time Melanie would go there on the weekends, but occasionally John came to Sedona. That particular weekend, John had a convention to attend with his company, so that's why he came up during the week. He wanted to see Melanie before he left town since they'd miss their weekend together."

"How far a drive is Phoenix from Sedona?" Kelly asked.

"John lived on the outskirts of Phoenix, about ninety miles from where Melanie lived. Depending on traffic, Melanie said it usually took her one and a half to two hours on average."

Kelly looked in Dan's direction and gave a slight nod, hoping he'd understand that she wanted him to segue into asking about Melanie's friends, especially Sally Gibson.

"Amanda, the last time we spoke, you told me about a conversation you'd had with Sally Gibson, a close friend of Melanie's."

"Yes, I remember. I'm afraid I might have made more out of it than what I should have due to my frustration over not being able to get any answers. I only realized that after Sally called to say she was sorry if she'd given me any false hope. She went on to say that she didn't think anything about it at the time because it wasn't unusual for Melanie to strike up a conversation with people she didn't know. I know this to be true. My daughter never met a stranger. She could have been friendly to a dozen people she didn't know on that day. Do you track them all down, invade their lives, and consider them suspect because Melanie was friendly to them? I don't know. I guess I'm grasping at any hope I can find."

Kelly thought it curious for Sally to have called Amanda. She knew it had to be after she was at Sally's house since Kelly was the one who told her about Mrs. Davies' conversation with Dan. "Did Sally call recently?" she asked.

"Yes, just yesterday, as a matter-of-fact. She asked how we were doing and apologized for not keeping in touch. The last time I saw her was when we went through the photo albums together. Before she left, she said she'd like to keep in touch and asked if she could stop by once in a while. I assured her that I'd enjoy her visits. When Sally and Melanie were kids, they were together all the time—not quite as much after we moved, but Melanie still spent more time with Sally than any of her other friends. I always liked Sally. I'm sure she was sincere in wanting to visit more, but people have busy lives, and before you know it, weeks, even months go by and you wonder where the time went."

"I know what you mean," said Kelly.

Dan continued. "Amanda, when you told me about Sally seeing Melanie in the coffee shop, there must have been something she said to make you feel that it might be important."

Amanda thought for a moment. "Sally said she waved at Melanie, but Melanie seemed to be in a serious discussion with this person and didn't notice Sally at the window. That stood out to me because, if she was just being friendly to a stranger, then why did it seem so serious? I asked Sally about it during our phone call and she said she should have used the word 'interesting' instead because it was nothing more than that, and she was very sorry if her misuse of words caused me to worry."

Kelly and Dan asked the Davies a few more questions about Melanie's other friends and acquaintances, and if Melanie ever indicated having a problem with anyone. "If there was a problem, she never let on to us," said Amanda, "but the last time I saw her, she did seem a little preoccupied and not as talkative as usual. When I asked her about it, she said she was just tired from being up most of the night watching movies, which she had been known to do on occasion. She loved old movies." Amanda looked out the window up toward the sky. "Since her death, I find myself wondering if she was troubled about something but didn't want to worry me."

Chapter Twenty-Seven

After Dan dropped Kelly off at her condo, she called Joe to tell him about their visit with the Davies.

"How did you feel when you left there? Do you still think Sally knows more than what she's willing to tell?"

"I'm not sure. Amanda Davies seemed satisfied with Sally's explanation after they talked on the phone yesterday, but something doesn't feel right to me."

"The fact that Sally felt the need to call Amanda right after your visit might have something to do with it."

"Yes, that's part of it. According to Amanda, she hadn't spoken with Sally since they went through the photo albums together—which was weeks ago—until she called yesterday."

"What's the other part?" asked Joe.

"I don't know. It's weird. Even though I think Sally knows more than what she's saying, I don't believe she realizes the importance of what she knows."

"Come again?"

Kelly laughed. "It's complicated, and I'm not sure you'll understand."

"Try me."

"Joe, I feel that Sally is innocently involved, and I strongly believe she's hesitant to discuss what she may or may not know because she's concerned she might wrongly implicate someone."

"Interesting."

"Doesn't make sense, does it?"

He chuckled. "Coming from you, it does. Maybe you should be talking to Gina."

"You might have a point."

"Seriously, Kelly, I've had hunches like that. When you feel it, you have to go with it, because sometimes all you have to go on are your gut feelings."

"Yeah, I suppose. Gina said something similar to me before she left town to attend her friend's wedding. Speaking of Gina, I need to go over to her condo tonight and check on her plants. I meant to do that this morning," Kelly brought Joe up to date on everything she and Dan had learned, and he told her that he thought the meeting with the Davies, and her visit with Sally, would prove more helpful than she realized. She said she'd talk with him more in a few days and was just about to hang up when he stopped her.

"Kelly, before you go, I want to let you know that I've firmed up my plans for next week."

"So, you're coming. Good!"

"Yeah. The timing couldn't be better. Dan called me yesterday and said that there was something he wanted to talk to me about, but he'd like to do it in person. I want to see him while I'm there, but I was more focused on spending most of my time with you. I told him I'd catch up with him mid-week."

Kelly was surprised. Dan hadn't mentioned anything to her about talking with Joe, or that there was something he wanted to discuss with him. "Joe, I was with Dan all afternoon. He never said a word about talking with you, or that you would be here next week."

"I know. I asked him not to. I wanted to tell you myself."

"Does he want your help with the Davies case?"

"I don't think that's the reason he wants to see me—at least he didn't indicate that—but I'm sure he wouldn't mind if I got involved ... that is, of course, if you're still okay with me helping."

Of course I'd like for you to be here in Arizona, working closely with me and sharing ideas! I just don't know if it would be a wise thing to do at this time. It would be so easy to allow myself to get involved with Joe, but I don't want it to be for the wrong reasons. Am I strong enough to be around him and prevent that from happening? I'm not sure, but I'll just have to make certain that I am.

"Why the pause, Kelly? It's your case. You're the one in charge. I take orders from you. You should love that!" he said jokingly.

"And don't you forget it," she teased back, feeling slightly less vulnerable. *That's the key: Keep things light and stay focused on the business at hand.*

Chapter Twenty-Eight

By the time Kelly decided to head over to Gina's apartment, the sun had already set. Since the moon was bright and the air cooled from the heat of the day, Kelly walked the modest distance to Gina's complex. One of the neighbors Kelly had met at the potluck was sitting out on his first floor patio sipping what appeared to be a brandy.

"A little late to be taking an evening stroll by yourself, don't ya think?" he said. "I saw you come from across the street. You're Gina's friend, aren't you?"

"Yes, I am. And if I remember correctly, you're Walter."

He smiled. "It's nice of you to remember my name. I'm afraid I've forgotten yours. Can't use my age as an excuse. I've always been bad with names, but I never forget a face."

Making her way to his patio, she extended her hand. "I'm Kelly. I came to the potluck with my friend Joe."

"Ahh, yes ... I remember now. Kelly, would you like to join me in a brandy?"

"Thanks for the offer, but I'd better take a raincheck. I'm on my way to Gina's ..." before she could finish, Walter interrupted her.

"She's not home. Gone out of town for the weekend. Some kind of celebration," he scrunched up his nose and rubbed his chin, "a wedding or something of that nature. Didn't she tell you?"

"Yes, I knew she was going out of town for a few days. She asked me to check on her plants and see if they needed watering."

"Oh, I see. Do you know if she has a boyfriend?"

"I don't believe so. At least she hasn't mentioned one to me. Why do you ask?"

"Saw a man over there last night. She's right across the parking lot from me on the second floor," Walter said, pointing to her unit, "but I guess you know that. Anyway, if she's coming or going and I'm on my patio, we always wave and holler greetings to each other. I'm usually out here in the mornings and evenings when it's not too hot."

Kelly looked across the small parking lot to Gina's unit, and she could see that Walter had a good view of the front door. The stairs were about six feet to the right of her unit.

"Could you tell if the man was knocking on her door?" Kelly asked, wondering if he might have been a salesman.

"I can't be sure, but it didn't look to me like his arm was raised to knock. As you can see, even with the street light on, if he knocked, but kept his hand close in front of him, it would be hard to tell."

Kelly looked around the complex where the lights were situated. "The street lights don't come on until later in the evening during the summer months," she said. "What time was it when you saw the man at her door?"

Walter thought a moment. "It was late, because I couldn't sleep and stepped outside to get some fresh air. I just finished watching the ten o'clock news. I poured myself a glass of water and then came outside, so it had to be between ten-thirty and eleven o'clock. That's why I wondered if it might have been a boyfriend. I can't imagine anyone else stopping by that time of night."

"Nor can I," said Kelly. "Walter, did anything else catch your attention, other than his being there that late?"

"No, not really. He wasn't there long. I was just about to holler to him and ask if he was looking for Gina when it appeared as if he was peeking in the window above her door. The shades are pulled so he couldn't see in anyway. Before I could say anything, my neighbors—the Wilsons—came home from dinner and a late movie, and when he saw them pull into the parking lot, he left. Maybe he was trying to locate a buddy of his and had the wrong building. Who knows?"

"Yeah, who knows. Well, it's been nice talking to you, Walter, but I'd better get going before it gets any later."

Walter looked at his watch. "I guess I'll go in now and get settled for the night. It won't be too much longer before my news comes on. You take care, ya hear?"

"I will, and you do the same."

Kelly walked across the parking lot to Gina's building and climbed the stairs to the second floor. She reached in her pocket and took out the key, but before she inserted it into the lock, she paused and looked around to make sure she was alone. As she stepped inside, she thought about the man who had been there the night before. Locking the door behind her, she searched for the light switch and turned it on. Everything seemed normal with the lights on. Walking through the living room she paused a moment to admire Gina's artwork before proceeding to the elephant plant in the corner of the room. The soil beneath the plant felt moist, so she knew Gina must have remembered to water it before she left town. Gina had also asked Kelly to check the plants surrounding the tub in the bathroom off her bedroom. She said it was a perfect spot to keep them since she always took showers and never used the tub. A large window was situated over the tub, and Gina mentioned that the afternoon sun shown through, giving the plants plenty of sunshine. Kelly was disappointed when she walked through the bedroom. She was hoping to see one of Gina's paintings in progress, but the easel was bare. There were a few completed paintings lined up on the floor against the wall opposite the bed—all were of Sedona's red rock formations. She was awestruck at how beautiful and accurate they were.

After checking the plants and making sure everything was in order, Kelly turned the lights off and locked the door on her way out. The full moon and the mild night air made for a nice walk home.

Chapter Twenty-Nine

Kelly spent hours that morning reviewing the files, but she didn't find anything else that appeared questionable from the other interviews. Feeling the need to see Sally again, Kelly decided to call her, and even though it was Sunday, Sally would agreed to meet with her.

"Hi, Sally, I'm glad you were able to see me today, especially on such short notice," Kelly said when Sally opened the door. "I promise not to take up much of your time." They sat in the living room, Kelly on the sofa facing Sally, who sat upright in the La-Z-Boy recliner. The smell of fresh coffee wasn't present as it had been the first time Kelly visited. Sally fidgeted with her hands and appeared uncomfortable.

"It's strange, you calling me when you did," Sally said. "I was debating whether or not I should call you."

"Oh? Does it have anything to do with the last time you saw Melanie in the cafe with the stranger? Or does it have more to do with your phone call to Mrs. Davies?" Kelly wanted Sally to know right off the bat that she knew about her conversation with Amanda.

"Is that why you wanted to see me, Kelly? To talk about my call to Mrs. Davies?"

"Why don't we start with why you were thinking about calling me?" Kelly suggested. "Is there something you thought of since I was here last that you feel might be helpful in solving your friend's murder?"

Sally didn't make eye contact. Instead, she stared down at her hands which were still fidgety. "Ever since Melanie's death, I think I've been in a state of denial. I began to rationalize my thoughts and concerns until they became reasonable explanations to me ..." She paused.

"Go on," Kelly urged.

Looking at Kelly, she said, "I don't know where to begin. I'm so confused about everything. Nothing makes sense."

"Let's start with the last time you saw Melanie alive. I believe that was in the cafe with the stranger."

"He wasn't a stranger."

"You mean it was someone Melanie knew all along?"

"I don't know if Melanie knew him or not prior to that day, and I don't know why she *would* have known him."

Kelly shook her head. "Now *I'm* confused."

"I know. Kelly, I've lied to myself to justify what I didn't understand until I fully believed the story I created. When you came to see me the other day, I started thinking about everything, and realistically, I knew that I no longer could believe what I'd been telling myself. At this point, I don't know what to believe."

"Tell me what you know and maybe I can help put the pieces together. Sally, who was the man you saw with Melanie?"

"I think it was my boyfriend's brother. No, I *know* it was him. I wasn't sure at first because I'd only met him once, and a lot of people look alike. The night after you were here, my boyfriend and his brother came over. I noticed a tattoo on his brother's arm. I remembered seeing the same tattoo on the man in the cafe: A large frog jumping out of—what looked like—a frying pan."

Kelly dug into her purse and took out a small spiral notepad. "Sally, what's your boyfriend's name?"

"Mark Kemenski."

"And his brother?"

"Andy."

"And you don't know why he would be seeing Melanie?"

"That's where it gets confusing. Melanie called me a couple of days before I saw her in the cafe. She said she needed to talk to me. She said it was important and it had something to do with Mark. I tried to get her to tell me over the phone, but she wouldn't. She insisted we meet so she could tell me face-to-face. She said that it was a serious situation and she wanted to make sure I knew about it in case she had to take matters further. We were planning on meeting the following week. I was very curious and wanted to see her sooner, but Melanie said she couldn't and the following week would be soon enough. I had a feeling that she didn't really want to tell me, but she felt she had to."

"Do you think she purposely wanted to wait a week in hopes the situation would resolve itself?"

"I don't know."

"Do you have any idea what Melanie wanted to tell you about Mark?"

"Not exactly. I certainly didn't at the time, but now the questions keep coming and the answers scare me to death. If I don't talk to someone, I'm going to explode!" Sally got up and paced back and forth. When she sat back down, she had tears in her eyes. "Melanie was my best friend. I don't want to believe what I'm thinking because, if it's true, then it means I might have contributed to her death."

As much information as Sally was giving, Kelly knew there was much more to come. She was anxious to hear all of it, but she had to be cautious not to rush Sally. She didn't want her to forget anything or become fearful and clam up.

Leaning forward in her seat, and in a softer voice, she asked, "Sally, why would you think that in some way you could have been responsible?"

Sally stared off into space, then as if she'd just realized the magnitude of what she'd said, she quickly responded. "You did say that you worked for a private investigator who was helping Mr. and Mrs. Davies, right?"

"Yes, that's correct."

"Since you're not a cop, can you promise me that anything I tell you will remain between the two of us—at least until you can prove whether it's true or not?"

"I will do my best, but I can't promise. Sally, I don't believe that you were directly involved in what happened to Melanie, but I think you have information that might lead us to who was."

"But what if I'm wrong?"

"The sheriff's department is investigating Melanie's death since she was murdered in their jurisdiction. If you're right, we'll have to share what you know with Sheriff Matt Gardner. But until then, and for as long as we can, Dan Mathews and I will keep what information you have between the three of us for now. Sally, you *have* to talk to me. I know you want to avenge your friend's murder, and you may be the only one who holds the key. If it turns out that someone you know *is* involved, is that the type of person you want to protect—someone capable of killing your best friend?"

Sally sat silently, holding back tears. "I can't say anymore right now. I need time to process my thoughts. I don't know what I think. I don't know what I believe. I only know there's a lot going on that doesn't make sense. I need a few days to sort it all out."

Kelly didn't want to leave—not now when she was so close to finding out what Sally knew. "Sally," she continued slowly, "tell me about Mark. What could Melanie have known that you didn't?"

Sally's cell rang. "It's Mark." She looked panicked. "I have to take it. He said he might come over this afternoon."

"Don't let on that I'm here," said Kelly.

Sally nodded in agreement. When she finished her conversation, she told Kelly that Mark would be there in thirty minutes. "Kelly, I promise I'll call you in a couple of days." She got up to walk Kelly to the door. "And I won't hold anything back. I just need a little more time to understand it myself."

As Kelly walked by the TV, she noticed a picture on the stand. It was of a man wearing a red cap. Realizing that he looked familiar, she picked up the picture and studied it. "Sally, who is this?"

"That's my boyfriend, Mark."

Chapter Thirty

Monday morning came too soon for Kelly. She was wakened—earlier than she would have liked—by the ringing of her cell. After meeting with Sally the day before, she hardly slept that night. What were the chances of Sally's boyfriend being the same person she met at Bell Rock? She couldn't be sure, because there were differences. The man in the picture wasn't wearing sunglasses and had a big smile, but he *was* wearing a red cap. She couldn't see "Huskers" on it because he was wearing it backwards, but just holding the picture sent an uneasy feeling through her.

When she'd gotten home from Sally's yesterday afternoon, she called Dan and brought him up to date. Next, she'd called Joe and they talked for almost an hour. He suggested that if she hadn't heard back from Sally by the end of the day on Monday, then *she* should call *her.* He told her to be careful not to give Sally too much time to herself, especially since they had no way of knowing what Sally might be saying to her boyfriend. Kelly agreed.

The clock on the nightstand read seven a.m. *Who in the world would be calling me this early?* She rubbed her eyes and reached for the phone.

"Hello?"

"Kelly, it's Sally. I know it's early, but I need to talk to you. I was hoping you could meet me this morning before I have to be at work."

"Yes, of course." Wide awake now, Kelly jumped out of bed. She heard the urgency in Sally's voice. "Just tell me where and when." Sally worked at Safeway so they agreed to meet at eight in the parking lot. Sally asked Kelly to park next to her Prius, and then she'd get in Kelly's car and they'd drive around to the back of Safeway where they could talk without being noticed. It all seemed a little mysterious to Kelly, but she did as Sally asked.

"Thank you for meeting me," Sally said once Kelly had shut the car off. "I know it was short notice, but I really needed to talk to you before I lost my nerve."

"I'm glad you called, Sally. Now, please tell me anything and everything you know that I don't."

"I don't know where to begin."

"Well, I have a few questions of my own, so why don't I start things off?" Sally took a deep breath and nodded her head. "How long have you known Mark?"

"I met him about a year ago when I was exploring Bell Rock. I usually hike different areas closer to my home, but since Melanie liked Bell Rock so much, I decided to check it out. Anyway, as I was getting ready to leave, I ran into Mark. He was very friendly and asked a lot of questions. He mentioned that he'd just moved to Sedona from Nebraska and wasn't very familiar with the area. We talked for a while, and then he suggested we go to lunch. He said I seemed to know a lot about Sedona, and he wanted to learn more. Normally, I wouldn't go off with someone I'd just met, but I felt comfortable with him. I even felt a little chemistry between us, so I took him up on his offer. That's how it started, and we've been dating off and on ever since."

"What do you mean by 'off and on'?" Kelly asked.

"Mark is very open about most things, but he's secretive when it comes to his work. He told me he works undercover for the government, and his position was such that he couldn't talk about it to anyone. I wasn't allowed to ask questions. Other than that, we had a great relationship, so one day I suggested that we live together. Mark said we couldn't until he completed the assignment he was working on, otherwise it would complicate matters. There'd be times he would leave town without notice and be gone for days. If I couldn't reach him, then I knew he was doing something for the government and he'd contact me when he was back in town."

Kelly thought that if the man she met at Bell Rock was the same man in the photo by Sally's TV, then the story he'd told her was very different from the one he'd told Sally. She wondered if either version was true. "Sally, does Mark have any cousins or other family members living in Sedona besides his brother, Andy?"

"Not that I know of. Why?"

"Just thought I'd ask." Kelly didn't want Sally to know that Mark might be the same man she met at Bell Rock, at least not until she heard what Sally wanted to tell her. "Sally, why don't you tell me what you were hesitant to say yesterday?"

Sally took another deep breath and slowly began. "Melanie and I met for lunch the week before she called to say that she needed to talk to me about Mark. She said something during lunch that I didn't give much thought to until recently." She paused.

"And what was that?" Kelly asked, wanting to move her along before she had to leave and clock-in for work.

"Melanie asked me if I had ever noticed Mark being unusually friendly or flirtatious, or if he had ever done anything to make me feel uncomfortable in our relationship. I laughed and said of course not. What a strange thing to ask, I said."

"How did Melanie respond?"

"She said, 'Don't mind me. It's just that I don't know much about Mark and I want to make sure you're happy.' I dismissed it at that until she called the following week, wanting to talk to me about him. When she indicated that it was important, I began to wonder what she knew that I didn't."

"Did you ever talk to Mark about your conversation with Melanie?"

"No, I didn't want to upset him for no reason, and I still had no idea what Melanie wanted to talk to me about. But after she died, I began to feel conflicted and confused about him. I kept wondering what she wanted to tell me, and I kept thinking about seeing her with Andy. I knew she didn't know him, and I couldn't understand why he was there with her. I had all kinds of crazy thoughts go through my head. I asked myself the same questions over and over. Did Mark find out Melanie knew something about him that he didn't want me to know? Did he ask Andy to meet with her to persuade her not to tell me? Why was Melanie killed? Did it have anything to do with what she knew? The questions kept coming. Then I'd snap out of it and tell myself that those things only happen in the movies. I would concentrate on not letting my imagination and thoughts run wild. I even made excuses when I noticed a difference in Mark's behavior. I started to justify everything. If I allowed myself to think that the man I loved could be involved in any way with the death of my best friend, then what kind of friend does that make me? Could Mark have been so horrible a person, and me so blind, that my friend ends up dead? Kelly, please find out what really happened to Melanie and prove Mark's innocence so I can quit having these terrible thoughts."

"Sally, no matter what happens, the only way you'll have any peace is to know that you did all you could to help resolve it." She noticed tears cascading down Sally's cheeks. She paused and took a clean tissue out of her purse and handed it to her. She waited a moment before continuing. "How was Mark different after Melanie's death?"

"He didn't go to the funeral with me, which I thought was strange, because he knew I needed the support. He said he wasn't feeling well, but I didn't believe him. When he came over later he seemed fine. All I wanted to do was talk about Melanie and try to understand how this could have happened. I wanted him to comfort me, but he didn't. He even seemed annoyed that I was so emotional."

"Was this behavior out of character for him?"

"Oh, yes. He had always been very caring and loving toward me. But when I needed his support the most, all he seemed interested in was knowing who attended the funeral. He didn't seem to care about how I felt, or that Melanie suffered a brutal death. He didn't want to listen to me talk about my friend. He made some excuse about having to get up early, and then he left. Days later, I brought it up to him and told him how it made me feel. His response was that it made him uncomfortable because he'd never seen me so emotional, and he didn't know what to say. After that, anytime I brought Melanie's name up, he became agitated and changed the subject. At the time, I wondered if his behavior might have something to do with the type of work he does, so to keep peace, I never mentioned Melanie's name again. It's put a strain on our relationship. Maybe that's why I've begun to look at things differently."

"In what ways are you looking at things differently?" Kelly asked. She felt that in some way, Mark had to be involved, because there were too many coincidences. She was hoping Sally would give her something more concrete to go on.

"I'm trying to be more objective and not let my feelings for Mark cloud my judgment. I have too many unanswered questions but, at the same time, I'm not willing to accept that Mark could be involved. He hardly knew

Melanie. Why would he want to hurt her? I don't know why Andy was with Melanie, but maybe he had something to do with it. He was the last person I saw her with."

Kelly debated whether to tell Sally about her encounter with the man at Bell Rock, but she decided it might be best to leave that for another day. She wanted to talk to Mark first and find out for herself if he was the same person. She wanted to know why—among other things—he told her a story about a cousin that obviously wasn't true. She also wanted to know why he began to approach her when she found the knife. Knowing that she might be dealing with a murderer—and if he murdered once, he could do it again—she'd have to be careful and not take any risks.

"Sally, how can I get in touch with Mark?"

"That will be difficult. He uses a disposable and non-traceable phone, which he told me was due to his line of work. Once a month, he changes phones and has a new number. When he stopped by yesterday, he told me it was time for a new phone and he'd call me once he knew the number."

"Where does he live?"

"I don't know. Again, he said that while he was working undercover, he wasn't at liberty to divulge that. He promised to bring me over to his place when he's finished with this particular assignment."

"Do you know where his brother lives, and do you have *his* phone number?"

"No. I'm sorry, Kelly, but I don't have a clue." Sally looked down at her watch. "I have to go."

"Okay. I'll be in touch."

"One more thing, Kelly. A couple of weeks ago, Mark was supposed to come over for dinner. He was an hour late and seemed distracted. He hardly touched his food and left early. I don't know what that was about—I've learned not to ask—but he wasn't himself."

Kelly's realization was instant: *A couple of weeks ago? That's just about the time I found the knife.*

Chapter Thirty-One

Gina was due back Sunday evening, but on the drive home from Sally's, Kelly realized she hadn't heard from her yet. *I wonder if I should check on the plants. I probably should. I expected her to be home last night, but anything could have happened. Maybe her friends talked her into staying an extra day.*

Joe told Kelly his flight should get into Flagstaff around five p.m. By the time he got his luggage, rented a car, and drove to Sedona, he would be there around 6:30, give or take a few. Kelly thought about calling him before he left for the airport to tell him what had happened since their phone conversation last night, but she decided to see Dan first and tell him about her morning with Sally. She also thought it would be better to tell Joe in person when he wasn't distracted by packing and getting to the airport. When he got in would be soon enough.

On the drive to Flagstaff, Kelly had plenty of time to reflect. She felt Mark was definitely involved in some way. Then there's his "cousin," who she now knows could be his brother. Was he the person she saw by her car in the parking lot when she met Gina for lunch?

Could Mark or Andy be the man who was at Gina's door late at night? But why Gina? How would they know her? There were so many things she wanted to talk to Dan about, and she hoped she'd have more answers by the time Joe arrived. She was glad she'd decided to go to Dan's office rather than try to explain everything over the phone.

"I'd say you had quite a weekend," Dan said, excited to hear all the news.

"Interesting and informative to say the least," Kelly countered. "Our biggest problem right now is finding Mark."

"Shouldn't he be getting in touch with Sally pretty soon?"

"I would think so. At least that's the way it's worked in the past, according to her. My concern is if Mark *is* the same person I saw at Bell Rock, then he's guilty of something, and he knows we're onto him. There's no telling what he'll do now. If he doesn't get in touch with Sally, then I don't know how we'll find him."

"He's certainly not making it easy, but we have our ways," said Dan. "First thing I'll do is have Jen check all the airports, train stations, and bus depots in the state to make sure he isn't planning on leaving town. And let's hope Mark Kemenski is his real name. I'll have Jack run a search on all Mark Kemenskies and see what we come up with."

"I guess I'd better give Matt Gardner a call and bring him up to date."

"Hmm ... Kelly, let's sit on it a day. Call the sheriff and tell him you have some information and you'll be in tomorrow to go over it with him."

"I think he'll be anxious to find out what I know. What if he insists I tell him over the phone—or worse yet—suggests coming over? After all, he did let me take the files home."

"Just tell him you're working with me on another matter and you won't be back until tonight. All you have to go on right now is what Sally told you, and she's not even sure of what she thinks she knows."

"Yeah, and I did tell Sally we'd try to keep it between us for a while, but that was before she called this morning. Matt trusted that I'd alert him to any information I found, and I'm sure that's why he felt comfortable with me having the files. It's obvious that Sally knew a lot more than what she stated in her interview, although I don't think she realized the importance of it at the time."

"Yes, Kelly, but all the sheriff is going to see is that she lied in her interview. Let's give Jen and Jack time to do some research and see what they can find out. Then maybe you'll have more concrete information for the sheriff, which might take the focus off of Sally lying. Kelly, I've been in this business a very long time, and too many times I've seen law enforcement have tunnel vision. I think you're right. I think Sally is innocent. Let's gain insight into Mark and take the spotlight off Sally. By learning more about him, it will help substantiate our suspicions. We may even find that he has a prior criminal record. I'd also like to know more about Andy and what role he might have played in all this."

"I see your point. A lot of what we have is hearsay and speculation. Matt could think Sally knows more than what she's saying, and he might even believe that she was an accomplice."

"That's right. Kelly, my position is different from yours. I represent the Davies. I don't have an obligation to the sheriff at this point, but you're caught in the middle. You work for our firm now, but you found the knife and you agreed to help the sheriff. You could help Sally, and even the sheriff, by waiting at least another day to see what we find out."

Kelly thought over everything Dan had said and realized that there was a lot she needed to learn about the private investigative industry. "Alright, I agree. It's still early in the day, and we have time to discover new information before tomorrow. Besides, I'd like to fill Joe in on what we know thus far and get his take on it."

Chapter Thirty-Two

No sooner had Kelly walked into her condo when she received a call from Gina. "Hi, Gina. Are you back home now?"

"No, but I'm on my way. I should be in Sedona shortly."

"I'm glad you called," said Kelly. "I knew you were supposed to be home last night, so when I didn't hear from you, I started to get a little concerned. I hope you had a great time, and I hope everything went well."

"Too well, and that's why I stayed another day. Kelly, I had good intentions and planned to call you last night. As it turned out, my friends talked me into staying an extra day so I could go to a rock concert with them. The last time all of us did that was when we were in college. We had a blast! By the time the concert let out and we got back to the house, it was just too late to call."

"No problem. I figured it was probably something like that. I would have called and left a message if I hadn't heard anything by this afternoon. I wondered if I should go over and water the plants, but since you'll be there in a little while, I won't worry about it. Let me know when you're back and I'll bring the extra key over.

If I don't do it right away, I'm afraid I'll misplace it and never think of it again." Kelly laughed, "I'm okay for a day or two but after that all bets are off."

"Sounds good. I'll give you a call when I get home—which should be around five o'clock unless I hit traffic."

"Okay. I promise not to stay. I'm sure you'll be tired from your trip, and Joe might be coming over later." Kelly wanted to tell Gina about her visits with Sally, but she mostly wanted to ask if Gina had any idea who might have been looking in her door a few nights ago.

"I didn't know Joe was in town," said Gina.

"He isn't—at least not yet. His plane gets in to Flagstaff around five, and by the time he gets his luggage, rents a car, drives to Sedona, and checks into the motel, it could be between seven and seven-thirty before he gets here. If it's any later than that, he might decide to wait until morning to come over."

"As long as he knows you're still up, I can't see him waiting that long to see you," said Gina.

A smile came over Kelly's face. She looked forward to seeing Joe, but this time she was especially anxious to see him, because she wanted to tell him everything Sally had discussed with her that morning. "Gina, in case you're right and Joe does come over tonight, I doubt he'll get here before seven o'clock. Why don't I give you time to unpack and relax a little, and I'll come over sometime after six?"

"That sounds good. Oh, by the way, how were the plants?"

"They were, and should be, fine, unless I killed them by watering too much."

"Thanks again, Kelly, for keeping an eye on things. I really appreciate it."

Thinking about the conversation she had with the neighbor, Kelly decided not to wait until Gina got home to tell her about the man Walter had seen at her door the other night. She wanted Gina to know about him so she could be careful, just in case he showed up again. "Gina, we've never talked about this, and it may seem like a strange question to ask right now, but do you have a boyfriend?"

Gina laughed. "It only seems strange that you couldn't wait until I got home to ask. Since moving to Sedona, I haven't met anyone yet who I'd seriously like to date. Why? Do you have someone in mind?"

"No, but I do have a reason for asking. I ran into your neighbor, Walter, when I went over to check on the plants. He was outside on the patio having a nightcap. We talked for a while and he mentioned seeing a man at your door the night before."

"Really? I have no idea who that could have been. Maybe I have a secret admirer," she teased. "Did Walter say what time he saw him?"

"He said he watched the evening news and then went to bed, but he couldn't sleep so he got up and stepped outside to get some fresh air. He thought it was close to eleven because the late news ended at ten-thirty."

"That's odd."

"Yeah, I thought so, too. That's why I asked if you had a boyfriend. I even wondered if it could be an ex-boyfriend who didn't know you were out of town. Then I thought it unlikely he'd stop by that time of night without calling first."

"Kelly, did Walter seem concerned?"

"Not really. I think he was more curious than anything. He wondered if it could've been a boyfriend or just someone who was lost and had the wrong address."

"I bet that's all it was. The units are so similar, he probably went to the wrong one."

"I didn't want to worry you, but I felt I should bring it to your attention in case he comes back."

"No, I'm glad you told me. I'll keep a watchful eye, but I'm not too concerned. Our neighborhood is pretty safe."

"Well, that may be, but I feel better having told you. I'll see you later, Bye."

"Thanks, Kelly."

Chapter Thirty-Three

As Dan had suggested, Kelly called Sheriff Gardner to let him know she had some information to share with him and would stop by his office before the end of the day on Tuesday. He asked questions, but she told him that someone was at the door—a little white lie—and she'd see him the next day.

Joe should be on his way to Flagstaff by now. I'm sure he'll call once he gets the rental car and is headed for Sedona. I think I'll make some finger sandwiches and slice up some cheese, just in case he hasn't eaten. Gina's right. I know Joe's not going to wait until morning to come over. He's as anxious to talk to me about the Davies case as I am to tell him about Sally Gibson. Kelly looked at her watch, then at the interview folders strewn across the table and sofa. *I have just enough time to straighten this place up and get in the shower before going over to Gina's.*

Joe called to let Kelly know he was on his way. "If you don't mind, I'd like to stop by your place before I check into the motel. I should be there by six-thirty."

"That sounds great, Joe, but I have one quick errand. I told Gina I'd bring her spare key by some time after six. I'll try to be back before you get here, but if

I'm not, please wait. I shouldn't be long."

"Familiar territory to me," Joe teased. "I've been left on a doorstep many a time."

Kelly laughed. "I doubt that." She told him not to worry about eating because she'd made some finger food and they could munch on it with a glass of wine while she brought him up to date on everything. She had a call coming in so they said good-bye. It was Gina.

"Hi, Kelly. I just walked in the door, so I'm a little later than I thought I'd be. Can you give me about thirty minutes to unload the car, put a few things up, and change into something more comfortable?"

"Sure. I'll stop by closer to six-fifteen and give you the key. I won't be able to stay and visit because I'm expecting Joe to be here around six-thirty."

"Would you rather bring the key over tomorrow afternoon? I'll be home from the center by then, and I'd love to tell you about my trip and catch up with you."

"I have a commitment tomorrow, and it looks like I could be busy most of the week. Why don't I touch base with you in a couple of days and we can see what our schedules look like then? But I'll bring the key by tonight, that way I'll have one less thing on my to-do list."

"Sounds good, Kelly. If I don't hear the doorbell, then please use your key and let yourself in. I might be in the bedroom still unpacking and putting things away, or changing my clothes."

"Okay. See you shortly."

After tidying the condo and making sure everything was in its proper place, Kelly was out the door and on her way to Gina's. It was still hot outside, but there was a slight breeze, so she walked the short distance. As she passed Walter's place, he opened the patio door and greeted her.

"Saw you coming this way so I thought I'd say hi. Guess you're on your way to Gina's."

"Hi, Walter. I *am* on my way to Gina's, but only to return her key. I have someone coming over in a few minutes and I have to get back."

"Must be going around," Walter said with a wink and a smile.

"What's that?" Kelly asked, unsure of what he meant.

"Company."

"I'm sorry, Walter," she paused in her walk, "but I'm not following you."

"Don't mind me, I'm just having a little fun with you. When you said you had to get back, I figured you had a boyfriend coming over just like Gina did."

Kelly looked over at Gina's condo. "What do you mean, Walter?"

"Well, I guess that fellow I saw over there the other night really *is* her boyfriend."

An uneasy feeling swept through Kelly. "Why do you say that?"

"I saw him snooping around over there—at least that's what I thought he was doing—but then the door opened and he went in. I didn't see Gina, but she must have let him in."

She probably thought it was me. With her heart pounding, uneasiness was replaced with intense concern. "Walter, are you telling me that a man went into Gina's condo, and you think it was the same man you saw the other night?"

"Yup, that's about it. I wouldn't have seen anything had I not been refilling my hummingbird feeder. I'm usually not out until later in the evening, but the feeders were empty and the birds were hovering. I just went back inside when I saw you headed this way, so I thought I'd say hello."

"I'm glad you did. It's been nice talking with you, Walter," Kelly said as she turned to go. "I'd better be on my way if I'm to get home in time for my guest." She hurried now, anxious to find out what was going on, but she didn't want to alarm Walter.

"Hope Gina knows you're coming," he called after her. "You might want to knock before entering, if you know what I mean," he smiled.

As she rushed to Gina's, Kelly wondered what she was going to do when she got there. Since she only expected to be gone a few minutes, she didn't take her cell with her. She hadn't planned on needing it.

Chapter Thirty-Four

Standing at the bottom of the stairway, Kelly contemplated her every move, wondering who could be inside and what they wanted with Gina. She knew that Gina wasn't expecting anyone or she would have told her. Kelly knew she had to be careful, she sure didn't want to be the cause of any harm coming to Gina. Each step was taken cautiously so as not to make a sound. When she reached the top of the stairs, she walked slowly to Gina's door and placed her ear against it, hoping to hear something. It was eerily quiet. Slowly grasping the doorknob, she turned it gingerly and held her breath, praying the door wouldn't squeak. She peered inside and seeing no one, stepped in and carefully closed the door behind her. Kelly realized she may be in danger, and her instincts were to find anything that could be used as a weapon. She heard voices coming from Gina's bedroom and quickly picked up the closest thing to her, a skinny bronze statue about a foot tall. Taking care not to bump into anything, Kelly made her way to the bedroom but stopped short of the doorway. She wondered if Gina had been unpacking, and if the stranger had picked the lock and let himself in.

"Who are you?" the man kept asking.

"I told you. I'm Gina Sanders, and if I'm not who you're looking for, then why are you here?"

"Where's the woman who lives here?"

"I keep telling you, this is *my* place! I live here. I can't make that any clearer. If I'm not who you're looking for, then please leave or I'll call the cops"

"I'm looking for an attractive woman of medium height with a small build. She has long auburn hair. Now where is she? I've seen her come and go from here. I thought she lived here."

"Kelly?" Gina asked in a confused tone. "What do you want with Kelly?"

"Where is she?"

"I don't know."

"Tell me or I'll beat it out of you!" the man yelled.

"I'm calling the police ..." Just as Gina got the words out, Kelly could hear her being thrown against the wall. She stepped in front of the partially opened door and she could see, about ten feet from her, the man's back. He was leaning over Gina who was huddled in the corner with her hands over her head, trying to avoid his punches. Kelly didn't need to see the man's face to know who it was. Without hesitation, she flung the door wide, raised the statue up high, and let it come down as hard as she could on the back of his head.

"I'm here, Mark! I'm here!" she blurted. Dazed, he stumbled to get up. Before she could strike again, he grabbed her ankle and pulled her to the floor, causing her to drop the statue. "Gina, run! Get help!" Kelly yelled.

Gina made her way past Mark and ran into the kitchen. From the butcher block on the counter, she grabbed a large knife. Mark staggered into the living room clutching the statue Kelly had just used to hit him with. He had to stop Gina from leaving. Holding the knife in a position to strike, Gina yelled, "Get out of here or I'll use this!"

Bracing himself against the counter, Mark was still a little woozy. He waved the bronze statue and laughed. "I dare you to try," he said coldly.

Kelly ran from the bedroom and rushed to the front door, hoping Mark would follow her. When Gina saw her, she lunged at Mark with the knife, but he used the statue as a bat, and struck her on the wrist. Gina screamed with pain and the knife flew from her hand. It hit the floor in Kelly's direction and she grabbed it before Mark could.

Mark stood between Gina in the kitchen and Kelly by the condo door. "Give me the knife, or I'll bash your friend's head in," he threatened.

"Maybe so, but you have no guarantee that I won't stab you first," said Kelly.

"Look at your friend," Mark said, but Kelly kept her eyes focused on him. Out of the corner of her eye, she could see Gina doubled over in pain, holding her wrist. Kelly had to find a way to trick him into coming after her. He was closer to Gina, and she knew Gina wouldn't stand a chance if he decided to hit her with the statue. She *had* to engage him.

"Mark, she's not the one you want, *I* am. I'm the one who found the knife at Bell Rock. I'm the one who talked to your girlfriend, Sally. I know Melanie must have had something on you, something that could send you to prison for years. And I know she wanted to tell Sally before going to the police." Kelly took a step in Mark's direction, talking all the while. Gina seemed to understand what Kelly was up to and inched her way closer to the butcher block. "What did you do, Mark? Did you try to rape Melanie when she rejected your earlier advances? Did she have you pegged from the start, and is that what she was going to tell Sally? Did Melanie find out that you don't really work for the government? Was she going to blow your cover? Is *that* why you had to kill her? There has to be more. What are you hiding, Mark?"

"Shut up! You don't know what you're talking about, and you don't have proof of anything."

Kelly stayed focused on Mark's eyes and not the statue. She hoped he'd forget he was holding it. She kept talking and slowly took another step toward him. "If I don't have proof, then why are you so worried? You saw me dig up the knife at Bell Rock—the knife you used on Melanie. That's why you came after me, isn't it?"

She started to take another step, when he yelled, "Stay back! Stay back!" One arm, hand in a "Stop" position, was out in front of him. The other held the statue. Noticing where Gina was, Mark ordered her to get over by Kelly.

"Don't move, Gina," Kelly pleaded. "As soon as you move in front of him he's going to attack you."

"You think you're so smart," sneered Mark, standing straighter now. He seemed to be getting his strength back after the blow to his head. Kelly knew they didn't have much of a chance now. He was bigger and stronger than the two of them combined. Kelly knew he could strike Gina with the statue first and quickly attack her before she'd have a chance to plunge the knife into him. She had to act fast.

"Gina!" She hollered at the top of her lungs in an attempt to distract Mark. He wasn't fooled, but Kelly's adrenaline was pumping so hard that when he swung the statue at Gina, she ducked just in time, and Kelly was able to stab him in the back. He gasped and dropped the statue, but he didn't go down, and Kelly realized that she didn't get the knife in deep enough. Gina tried to go around him, but he grabbed her by the hair and yanked her to him. Now, Kelly didn't have a weapon or any idea of what to do. She knew Mark was hurt, but he was far from dead. She wasn't sure how incapacitated he might be. Gina tried to break free to grab the statue, but Mark beat her to it. With the knife still in his back, blood dripping on the floor, Kelly knew he had to be in pain, but nothing seemed to stop him.

Gina reached for the statue with her good hand, trying to take it away from him. If she couldn't get it, she knew he'd use it on her and Kelly. He let go of her hair to maintain control of his weapon, and Gina began to run. As Mark struck at her, Kelly jumped in between them and took the brunt of the blow to her arm. She'd decided that if she was going to die, she wasn't going down without a fight. She began kicking him in the groin and punching back. Gina screamed and looked for something to throw at him. At that moment the condo door flew open, and Joe ran in. Pulling Kelly out of the way, he began beating Mark with with his fist. Mark swung the statue at him, but Joe was too quick and grabbed it just in time. Before falling to the floor, Mark landed a few good punches of his own, including one to Joe's eye, chin, and shoulder. Joe continued to beat him until he could no longer move. Gina ran over to Kelly, to make sure she was okay, then sat on the floor beside her. Joe, catching his breath, went over to join them. After making sure they were both okay, he looked at Kelly and smiled.

"I knew you had to have a good reason for standing me up." Kelly playfully punched him in the arm. "Ouch! Don't you think I've been punched enough for one day?" He looked over at Mark. "I think he got the worst of it. I'll call the sheriff and an ambulance for this creep. I'll have them send a second one for you and Gina. I think you both need to be looked at. Then you can fill me in on what happened here."

Chapter Thirty-Five

They declined the need for an ambulance, but Kelly and Gina agreed to let Joe take them to the hospital to be checked by a doctor. Most of their injuries were surface wounds along with some deep bruises. They were each given a topical cream to help ease the pain. Kelly's arm was black and blue and very sore, but nothing was broken. Gina, on the other hand, suffered a broken wrist that had to be put in a cast. Once Mark was treated and conscious again, the sheriff was told he could interrogate him. An armed guard stood outside his door.

Before seeing Mark, Matt wanted to talk to Joe, Kelly, and Gina to find out what had happened at the condo. After explaining all the details of that terrifying encounter with Mark, Kelly told Matt about her visits with Sally and that she suspected Mark was responsible for Melanie's death.

"If Mark *is* responsible, I'm still not clear on why he felt he had to kill Melanie. There had to be much more to it than his flirtation. Dan's doing a background check on him, but I don't know if he's found out anything yet. Mark was very secretive about his past and present with

Sally, and he may not be using his real name. Hopefully you can get something out of him when you talk to him. I'll come by in the morning, and we can call Dan to see what he's learned."

"Kelly, if you had told me all of this as soon as you knew it, maybe tonight wouldn't have happened," the sheriff said, annoyed.

"Leave her alone," said Joe. "She's been through enough for one night. You wouldn't have anything if it wasn't for Kelly. Besides, she was waiting until tomorrow when she thought she'd have more information."

Kelly was quick to respond. "I understand your frustration, Sheriff, but even if you had known, there's no way you could have prevented tonight from happening. There's no way you could have known that Mark would be at Gina's."

"Yeah, maybe so, but I still should have known. You guys go home and take it easy. I'll talk to Mark. Kelly, I'll see you in the morning, and Joe—I guess I'll see you, too.

Before replying, Joe looked at Kelly. He certainly didn't want to upset her by being there if he wasn't wanted. Kelly smiled and nodded. "Yes, Sheriff, I will be there," he said.

"I don't know how much I'll get out of this jerk tonight, but if I don't hear what I want, I'll be here first thing in the morning. Why don't you both show up around nine o'clock, I should be back in the office by then. Gina, you take care of that wrist. If I have any more questions for you, I'll call."

"Thank you, sheriff," Gina nodded.

When Joe and Kelly took Gina home, they insisted on coming inside and helping her with cleaning up the mess caused by Mark. Gina tried to protest, but when she was reminded of having one useless hand, she relented and graciously accepted their offer. Kelly and Gina cleaned up the floor and righted the furniture that had been knocked over while Joe washed up the blood left by Mark. When they were through, Gina asked them to please stay awhile longer and have a glass of wine with her. "It's the least I can do to thank you for all your help."

"I'd like that," said Kelly.

Joe asked Gina where the wine and glasses were. He told them to sit and relax, and he'd get everything and pour the wine. Kelly and Gina sat on the sofa and Joe sat in the chair across from them. There was a moment of silence.

Sipping the wine, the realization of what almost happened that night hit Kelly full-force, and she teared up. "Gina, you were almost killed because of me."

"What're you talking about?"

"If it weren't for me, Mark never would have been over here. You could have died tonight! I'm so sorry to have put you through this."

"You listen to me, Kelly Murphy: You *saved* my life! You risked your own life for me. I don't know of anyone else who would have done that. You're a true friend! Do you remember when I said to you that I didn't know why you were in Sedona, but I felt for some reason you were meant to be here?"

"Yes, I do remember. You also said that maybe I was meant to be here to learn something from someone else, or they were to benefit from me."

"Kelly, if you hadn't been here, that knife may never have been found. A murderer would still be on the loose, and whether they have enough evidence or not, I'm convinced Mark is their man. I don't mind being roughed up a little to know that he'll never be able to harm anyone else."

"Gina's right," said Joe. He got up from the chair to join them on the sofa, sitting close to Kelly. "There's something else I want to say to you." Clutching her wine, Kelly looked into his eyes, not sure that she wanted to hear what he had to say. "Kelly, you couldn't be there for Tara. You couldn't save her. Even though there was nothing you could have done to help her, you've always carried guilt because you weren't there. Kelly, you were here for Gina. You were here for Sally and every other woman who might have been injured or, worse yet, died at the hands of Mark. You may have solved Melanie's murder, and you may have brought closure to the Davies family. Tara would be so proud of you."

Kelly looked down at the wine glass clutched between her hands and smiled. She felt Tara's spirit, sensed Tara with her and felt peaceful. And for the first time since her death, she believed it was possible to have closure.

Chapter Thirty-Six

It was late when they returned from Gina's. Kelly picked up her phone from the counter where she'd left it and checked for messages. There was a call from Dan, left hours earlier. She decided to chance that he'd still be awake and called him. Wanting Joe to hear the conversation, she put the call on speaker. Dan was shocked to hear what happened to Kelly and Gina and all that Mark had put them through. He was glad Joe had gotten there and teased him about always wanting to be a knight in shining armor. "What a night, Kelly! I'm thankful that you're all okay."

"Thanks, Dan. Me, too. I'm glad to be home. Right now, I feel as though I never want to leave, but I know I'll feel differently in the morning—at least I'd better, because the sheriff wants to see Joe and me at his office. Dan, did you find out anything on Mark?"

"Yes, and that's why I called earlier. Mark Kemenski *is* his real name. He has no prior arrests, outstanding warrants, or even a traffic ticket. He looks squeaky clean. However, looks can be deceiving. For the last five years, he's lived in Lincoln, Nebraska, but there's no current address. There's a Ralph and Emily Kemenski who own a farm ten miles outside of Lincoln. They may be his parents, and he could have been staying with them when he went back and forth. It also showed an Andy Kemenski living in Arizona, so he could be Mark's brother.

"Now here's where it gets interesting. Jen and Jack looked through old newspaper articles from the last two years in and around Lincoln. One and a half years ago, a young woman in her early twenties was raped, but the rapist was never caught. She gave a pretty good description, except for his facial features. She was attacked late at night in her bedroom. She couldn't see his face that well, so the sketch artist wasn't able to come up with a good composite. Then a little over a year ago, a sixteen year old was jogging near a wooded area close to her home when she was brutally attacked and raped. She was a gymnast physically fit and very strong. She fought hard, but she was no match for him, and that's probably why she was beaten up so badly. It happened in broad daylight, so she was able to get a good look at her attacker. Jen printed a copy of the artist sketch from the newspaper. The police have DNA, but unfortunately you know how backlogged they are with rape cases. It may not have been tested yet. There are so many rape kits unopened, still sitting on the shelf."

"That's interesting, because Sally said she met Mark about a year ago. If he's responsible for the rapes, it would make sense for him to leave town if a sketch of him was being shown on the local news and in the newspaper. If Melanie had reason to become suspicious of

Mark, she could have done her own research and come across something that concerned her."

"Kelly, I'd like to meet with you and Joe at the sheriff's office in the morning. I'm sure he'd like to have this information. You two and the sheriff have seen Mark. The three of you can look at the sketch of the rapist and tell if there's a possibility that Mark's the person they're looking for back in Nebraska. What time are you meeting with the sheriff?"

"Matt said he wanted to be at the hospital early to question Mark before he goes to the office, so we decided on nine o'clock."

Joe leaned closer to the phone. "Dan, Joe here. We still have you on speaker, but I wanted to ask you something. I think it's a good idea for you to be there in the morning, but is there a chance you'll be in Sedona long enough for us to talk about why you wanted to see me?"

"Definitely. I'm not sure when we'll be able to talk—that depends on the sheriff's course of action but I won't leave Sedona until we do. I know the sheriff will arrest Mark for what he did to Kelly and Gina, but—after questioning him and reviewing this information—we'll see if there's enough evidence to charge him with Melanie's murder. If that happens, I think the Davies need to know immediately. They've waited long enough."

"I agree," said Joe.

"Dan, I'll want to contact Sally right away, too, and bring her up to date on everything. I'm sure Matt won't have a problem with that, unless he thinks that Sally could have been involved."

"I don't think we'll have a problem proving Sally's innocence," said Dan. "Tell you what we can do, Kelly. When I go to the Davies, maybe you could see Sally at the same time, and then the three of us can meet for an early dinner."

"That sounds good to me," said Kelly, "but I'll leave right after dinner so you and Joe can discuss what you wanted to talk to him about." Before ending the call, they agreed on a time and place to meet. Joe still needed to check into his motel, so he left shortly after Kelly hung up with Dan, so she could rest and get some sleep. But he added that if she needed to talk, he was only a phone call away.

Chapter Thirty-Seven

Unable to get much out of Mark—other than he only went to Gina's to rob her and things got out of hand—Sheriff Gardner's frustration was obvious when Kelly and Joe arrived. Against Joe's advice, Kelly drove herself, but she waited for him before going inside. She thought about Sally and how she was going to break the news to her if it turned out that Mark was the rapist from Nebraska. Finding out you've been dating and sleeping with a rapist, and believing you were in love with him, is enough to cause nightmares, but how do you accept that your involvement with him may have cost your best friend her life?

Kelly believed strongly that the artist sketch Dan told her about would prove to be Mark. And after what he put her and Gina through the night before, she didn't need intuition to tell her he was the same person who killed Melanie.

While waiting for Dan to arrive, Kelly and Joe told Matt about their conversation with Dan. They said he'd be there shortly with the information he had obtained, including a copy of the newspaper sketch of the man who raped the two women. "After what you've told me, I'm glad Dan's coming here—it saves me a trip to Flagstaff. I'll be interested to see if Mark is the same man who's wanted in Nebraska. If he is, that will explain a lot. You can rest assured he'll be getting another visit from me as soon as we're through here. This time he'll know it's pointless to waste my time with fabricating the truth. If I can convince him we have enough on him to put him away for life, he might just give it up." Matt smiled and shook his head. "I don't know what the three of you did to him last night, but he obviously got the worst of it. He was still in pretty bad shape this morning."

The door opened and Dan walked in, carrying a folder under his arm. He went over everything he had with the sheriff. Kelly had chills when he showed the artist sketch: The likeness to Mark was undeniable. Matt called the authorities in Lincoln, Nebraska, and told them he thought he had their rapist, but that he may soon be arrested in Sedona for murder.

Kelly was relieved to hear Matt use the words arrested, murder, and Sedona, in the same sentence when talking about Mark. "Matt, are you confident there's enough evidence to charge Mark with Melanie's murder?"

"I think there will be. I didn't want to say anything before now and get everybody's hopes up, but his DNA is all over the bronze statue. I'm confident that when it's compared to the DNA on the knife, we'll have a match." Turning to Dan, he added, "Seeing what your firm dug up on him has erased any doubt I might have had."

"I'm glad we could be of help," said Dan. "I'll be on my way now. I want to see Amanda and Sam Davies and let them know what we found out. He turned to Kelly and Joe, "I'll catch up with you guys later." Kelly called Sally and left right after Dan to meet her on her next break. Joe stayed behind at the office.

"Sheriff, I seem to be free the rest of the day, would you mind if I tag along when you go to see Mark?" he asked.

"I think that's a good idea. Two can be more persuasive than one. Once I show him the sketch and tell him we know what he did in Nebraska—that we have DNA from the knife to prove he's the one who murdered Melanie—there's not much he can say. But I want to know more about his brother, Andy, and his involvement."

When they entered Mark's room, his bed was raised to put him in an upright position. He was more alert than the last time the sheriff saw him, but there wasn't a Perry Mason moment. He said nothing when presented with the evidence. There was no confession and he remained quiet, ignoring the two men, until his brother was mentioned.

"You leave Andy out of this. He didn't do anything wrong."

"Well, you see, Mark, I can't do that. He obviously was an accomplice. He was seen with Melanie in a cafe shortly before she was murdered," said the sheriff. The more Matt talked about Andy's involvement, the more defiant and protective Mark became. It was obvious the brothers were close, and the sheriff used their relation-ship to his advantage. Since Mark didn't know who Joe was, the sheriff insinuated that he was a detective with the police department.

"Joe, you stay here with this creep and find out what you can. I'll go arrest his brother."

"No, don't! I'll tell you whatever you want to know, just leave Andy out of this. I'm telling you, he knows nothing. He has no idea what I've done. He knows I lied to Sally about working undercover for the government, but he thinks it's because I wanted to impress her and didn't want her to know I was out of work. He thinks I left Nebraska because I lost my job."

"What kind of work does Andy do that he could support you for the last year?" asked Joe.

"I did odd jobs for him at a construction site. He's a building contractor."

"So why did he go talk to Melanie?" questioned the sheriff.

"I told him Melanie found out that I lied about my job and I was afraid she was going to tell Sally and ruin our relationship. Andy offered to speak to her and per-suade her not to say anything to Sally. I told him not to because I knew if he talked to Melanie, she might tell him that I came on to her. He's my younger brother and I've always looked out for him. He thinks I can do no wrong. I didn't know he talked to Melanie until after the fact. Not only did she tell him that I came on to her, but she said if someone hadn't come along, she thought I might have forced myself on her. She didn't use the word 'rape,' but I knew that's what she meant. Andy didn't believe her. He thought she was just saying it to try and break Sally and me up because she didn't think I was good enough for her. Sally was good for me. She believed everything I told her, and she thought I was somebody important. I couldn't let Melanie mess that up. I had to do something."

When they left Mark, Matt and Joe went to the construction site where he said they could find Andy. They both felt that Mark was telling the truth about Andy and that he probably didn't know what his big brother was up to, but they wanted to hear it from Andy.

Andy didn't look much like Mark—he was shorter and a little on the chubby side. When they told him what Mark was suspected of doing, Andy refused to believe them. They showed him the sketch, told him about the DNA, and said that Mark had all but confessed, but he shook his head in disbelief. They talked for quite a while and Joe even mentioned that Sally had begun to suspect that Mark might be involved in Melanie's death. Andy was trying to make sense of it all. He was mumbling different things, and then mentioned how the breakup of Mark's first real relationship affected him.

"He loved that woman more than life itself," said Andy. "All he talked about was when they were going to get married and have children, but it never happened."

"Why?" asked Joe.

"He had been out of town and came home a day early. He had flowers and a gift for her, but he found her in bed with his best friend. He never got close to another woman until he met Sally. Mark struggled with relationships after that, suspecting all women of cheating on him. He became agitated and angry whenever he talked about women. He told me he thought they were all out to use men. When he lost his job, I became worried about his mental state. He just wasn't himself anymore, and he'd disappear for days at a time without letting anyone know. A couple of weeks ago, he said he met a woman on Bell Rock and that he didn't trust her, because she had taken something that belonged to him. He watched her get into her car, but she took off before he could get to her. I don't know what that was all about, but he wouldn't let it go. He described the car to me, and every car that looked like it made me curious, because he would never tell me what she took. It didn't make sense to me, and only made me worry more about him." He looked at both men. "If you don't mind, I want to go see my brother. He may have done some crazy things, but I can't accept that he's capable of murder."

The sheriff was satisfied with what Andy had told them, and he and Joe left.

Chapter Thirty-Eight

When Dan, Kelly, and Joe met up again for dinner, there was much to discuss.

"How did Melanie's parents take the news?" Kelly asked.

"For the most part, I think they were relieved that someone was finally going to be held accountable. Amanda said she hoped this would start the healing process and bring the closure they so desperately needed."

"How did they feel when they learned it was Sally's boyfriend?"

"They were shocked but took it surprisingly well. Amanda even showed compassion for Sally. She said it was a horrible tragedy, and she felt it had to be very difficult for Sally. Speaking of Sally, how did your visit go?"

"It was excruciating. At one point, I even thought she was going to pass out. She was overcome with emotion, as you can imagine. Sorrow, anger, guilt, regret—all of it. She doubled over as if she were going to be sick, and said that she couldn't believe she loved someone so despicable."

"That's too bad, Kelly. I hope she'll be okay."
"Me, too, Dan."

"Are you okay, Kelly?" Joe asked.

"Yes. I'm just glad it's over with, and I hope I never have to deliver a message like that to anyone ever again. She was so distraught, and I felt sorry for her. I did suggest that maybe seeing a counselor would be helpful in working through her grief and guilt over Melanie and all the emotions she's having about Mark right now. Joe, what did you and Matt find out?"

Joe told them what they learned from Mark and then about their visit with Andy.

"Mark must have had a lot of rage building after his breakup to do what he did to all those women," said Kelly. "I think the break-up was the catalyst. He probably was prone to being a rapist anyway. A lot of men have their relationships end and don't become rapist or murderers, for that matter. I'm just glad he's off the streets."

"I agree," said Joe.

"That's probably why he told Sally he was an undercover agent and had to be out of town at times. He could do crimes against women and Sally would never know. Then he could go back to her and pretend to be a respectable citizen," Kelly said.

They continued to talk through their meal. After dinner, Kelly excused herself so Dan could talk with Joe, but Dan asked her to stay. "Kelly, I realized that what I want to talk to Joe about will also affect you so, as my assistant, I'd like you to stay and hear what I have to say." Confused and not sure what she should do, Kelly turned to Joe. Dan spoke before Joe could say anything.

"Knowing Joe as I do, I don't think he'll mind if you're a part of the conversation," he assured her.

"I have no idea what you're going to say, Dan, but Kelly, he's right. I would like for you to stay."

Dan continued, "Joe, remember when I told you that ever since Tom retired, I've given some thought to my own situation?"

"Yeah, I remember. Dan, you're not seriously thinking about retiring, are you?"

"I told you how Joan's been longing to travel, but I've always been too busy. Well, I don't know how much time either one of us has left, and I'm no longer willing to assume that there will always be a tomorrow. A couple of weeks ago Joan found a lump in her breast and had to have a biopsy. Thankfully, it turned out to be benign. It scared the heck out of me, and it made me appreciate the support she's always given me. All of our married life, Joan has taken a back seat to my career. I'm not willing to put her through that anymore. It's time she got to see this beautiful country in the way she's always wanted. So, I've decided to sell my interest in the business—which is pretty substantial since Tom retired. Joe, I'd like you to consider taking it over." For a moment, Joe was at a loss for words. Kelly remained silent.

"Wow, Dan, I don't know what to say. I appreciate your trust and confidence in me—especially knowing you wouldn't sell to just anyone—but it's a lot to consider. After all, I have my own business, too."

"I realize that, Joe. I know it's not something you can decide on right away. All I ask is that you give it serious consideration. I don't know of anyone I'd rather see take over my interest and senior partnership in the firm than you. But, there's one stipulation," he paused as if waiting for a response.

"And that is ..."

"I have a new assistant who has proven herself to be quite worthy." Dan looked at Kelly and smiled. "Her position is not negotiable. She's part of the deal."

Joe leaned back in his chair and roared with laughter. He reached over and put his hand on Kelly's. "Dan, the opportunity wouldn't interest me near as much without your worthy assistant."

Kelly pulled her hand away and put both hands on her hips. She was no longer speechless. "Do I have a say as to whether or not I want to work for anyone other than you, Dan?"

By now, Dan had a good idea of how Kelly liked to give Joe a hard time. "I suppose you do, but I don't know of anyone—other than myself of course—who would be better to work for than Joe."

"Well, I'll be the judge of that," she said sternly, but she couldn't hide the smile.

Joe grabbed her hand again and squeezed it tightly as he looked into her eyes. "Kelly, it looks like we have a lot to talk about." Then he turned his attention to Dan. "Dan, I will seriously give this a lot of thought, and I'll be in touch as soon as I know something. I appreciate the circumstances that brought you to this life-changing move. I know it wasn't an easy decision. Thank you for considering me. It means a lot."

They left the restaurant together, and then Dan went his way and drove back to Flagstaff. Joe walked Kelly to her car. "You've had a long day," he said, "so I won't bother you tonight with my thoughts, but how about breakfast in the morning?"

"Only if you let me cook it," she insisted. "We'll be more comfortable talking without the noise and interruption of a restaurant."

"Tell me when and I'll be there." He reached for the door just as she did. As their hands touched, their eyes locked. He pulled her to him and kissed her gently. She didn't resist.

THE END

About the Author

Debby Arthur Warner, a mystery writer from Grand Junction, Colorado, enjoys spending her spare time in the Smoky Mountains of Tennessee where her second book *Four Keys and a Cabin* takes place. Her unique writing style creates a character that will remain with you long after the story ends. "I begin my story as revealed to me through my characters, and at that moment, I'm unaware of what's going to happen. When my hand moves, the pencil writes, and the journey continues through completion. I know only what I'm supposed to at the time of each writing."

In the sequel to *Only by Chance in Cripple Creek*, Debby brings back her colorful characters, Kelly and Joe, in *Sedona's Deadly Secret*.

www.ingramcontent.com/pod-product-compliance
Lightning Source LLC
Chambersburg PA
CBHW070953120726
47910CB00004B/1217